DRUG GANG

NEIL WALKER

First published worldwide by System Addict Publishing in
2017

This edition published worldwide by System Addict
Publishing in 2018

Copyright © Neil Walker 2017

NEIL WALKER

By the Same Author

Drug Gang Vengeance: Drug Gang Part II

Drug Gang Takedown: Drug Gang Part III

NEIL WALKER

Dedicated to Jean Yarr, Lily Yarr,
Cecil Yarr and Mary Jane Johnston.

NEIL WALKER

CONTENTS

"It's not what happens that counts,

it's how you react."

Bruce Lee

NEIL WALKER

DRUG GANG

NEIL WALKER

NEIL WALKER

Chapter One

Life is brutal. At least that's what John thought. Of course, he hadn't always had such a dark and bleak outlook. His time in Manchester had changed him.

He had seen things he could not unsee and been part of things he would never be able to get out of his mind, no matter how much he wanted to.

The English winter could be merciless and after three days of relentless rain, the clear sunny morning came as a welcome reprieve, not that the sun brought with it warmth. There remained a chill in the air, but John was way past caring about being cold or indeed about his personal welfare in general.

Self-loathing was on the agenda for the foreseeable future and he found it hard to imagine a way past it.

At this point, he wasn't even sure who he hated more, himself or them. Without a doubt though, he was at an all time low. Never before had his life been filled with so much negativity.

He had been wandering aimlessly around the grounds now for almost an hour and decided it was time to stop. Slumping down on to the moist February grass, he lay back, staring up into the clear sky.

A week had felt like a lifetime, every minute feeling like an hour, every hour a day. Sleep had eluded him for the most part and when he had slept, his dreams had been vivid and horrific enough for him to be fearful of drifting off again.

No rest for the wicked, so they say.

His intention that day had been to clear his head, find some space, but there was no escape. How can you escape from your own conscience, the reality of your own actions?

He looked endlessly into the sky - not seeking redemption or forgiveness - merely striving for one second of peace, one second where he could forget what he had done, what he had been a part of. It would never come though and deep down he knew it.

For the first couple of days he had tried to rationalise what had happened, make himself believe there was no way round it, that it had to be done, that it was - in some twisted way - the right and noble thing to do. He could only kid himself for so long, however.

The way forward was beyond unclear and thinking about the future was more than he could bear. This forced him to regress, to go back step by step and think about all that had happened.

He tried to pinpoint the change - the moment when he became the kind of person capable of such actions. Which step had been the step too far?

After all, he had been doing things that a lot of people would be ashamed of, or would never be a party to, for some time. He had pulled away from normal life and embraced his new lifestyle all the way, finding it easier to run from reality and the daily grind, than deal with it and come to terms with it.

And now this. This is where he had ended up, lying on his back, trying to forget himself.

Could it all have been different, or was it all inevitable after that one fateful day when he took the first step?

It had only been eight months, though it seemed so much longer, only eight months since he returned from Australia, only eight months since it all began...

NEIL WALKER

Chapter Two

It was a bright July day, without a cloud in the sky, certainly warm enough to draw the English sun-worshippers out of their houses to take advantage. For John it didn't feel like much. He had just flown in from an Australian winter filled with hotter days than this British summer.

The twelve months between the summer of 2000 and this summer of 2001 had been the best time of John's life. He had loved his international adventures, but now they were over and the greenery and mild summer heat only served to drive home that unpalatable reality.

They had been driving through scenic green countryside for around ten minutes now and there weren't many signs of life, bar the occasional farm animal and a run-down cottage they had passed a few miles back. John was feeling slightly nervous about what lay ahead and more than a little curious, so he was keen to get this over with.

"Nearly there?" he asked, without turning his head away from the window.

"Couple of minutes," was Michael's reply.

This was the first conversation there had been in the car for almost half an hour. Michael had made some brief small talk with Sanjay when they first got in and introduced John to him, but that was about it.

John wasn't sure if Sanjay was merely quiet or mean and moody, or if Michael just didn't feel like talking. He was like that - sometimes the life and soul and other times couldn't be bothered saying a word.

Sanjay didn't strike John as a very jovial type though. He looked like the kind of nightclub bouncer who wouldn't say much, but would have the simmering potential for violence that puts people off causing trouble.

He certainly wouldn't have been out of place in a nightclub doorway, around six foot four in height, a good couple of inches taller than John and with a build that would make him a boxing heavyweight.

Indeed, he reminded John of a large Asian bouncer who worked at The Jewel Bar in Belfast, or at least did the last time he had been there.

The car slowed as they approached the tall black metal gates and Sanjay used a remote control to open them electronically. A small gold plaque attached high on one of them announced that they were entering 'Nathan House'.

As they rolled up the driveway, John couldn't fail to notice the size of the grounds contained around the main building, which were huge, with grass and greenery stretching back for what seemed like miles.

And the building itself could only be described as a mansion. Very impressive, in keeping with the standard set by the Mercedes-Benz they had been driven there in.

Michael hadn't told him much and in fairness John hadn't asked too many questions, except for confirming beyond any doubt that the work he would be doing would not be sales. "Anything but sales," he had said, although now he was picturing himself in a butler's uniform, polishing the Mercedes.

Maybe he should have asked more questions. Such was his dread of the thought of going door-to-door again, or entering another soul-destroying call centre environment, however, that the words, "I know a guy who might have some work for you," were enough to bring about an extended stop over in England.

Indeed, his last few weeks on the Sunshine Coast had been marred by the thought of returning to his bleak employment situation in Belfast. He had been assured that he would have a position waiting for him with Exodus Promotions, selling people discount cards for bars and restaurants.

It had been bearable when it was to raise money for his travels, but if he went back to it now, he would just be a person with a tedious job, working to pay the bills on commission-based income.

As they walked through the main doors, they entered a majestic hallway with polished wooden floors, a chandelier hanging from the extremely high ceiling and antiques scattered around liberally.

Michael tapped John on the shoulder as they proceeded up the carpeted staircase.

"Gum?"

He held out a packet of sugar-free mint gum, which looked as if it had been in his pocket for some time, offering John a piece.

John shook his head.

"Just one thing mate - be honest."

Michael paused for a second to put a piece of gum in his mouth.

"If you're honest with him he'll love you. Just relax and have a chat with him, okay?"

John nodded and Michael patted him on the back.

The idea of being honest in an interview was a novel one for John. He was a master of rhyming off exactly what interviewers wanted to hear, telling them about how he was self-motivated, but happy to work alone or in a group. How he was keen and enthusiastic, with a real positive attitude. Of course, he would invariably have to confess his major fault - being too much of a perfectionist.

John was always confident he'd get the job once he got to the interview stage, although after he was fired from the call centre, interviews had not exactly come thick and fast.

There was something about the words 'Reason for leaving - fired', which didn't exactly get him on the shortlist. Hence the door-to-door job, who would hire anyone willing. Commission-only payment made it worth their while giving anyone a try.

"It's just here," said Sanjay, as they reached the top of the staircase.

It was the second door along a lengthy hallway and Sanjay pointed to it, letting him know that it was the one. He and Michael continued along the hall and John knocked the door, all set to meet the man who could save him from his employment crisis.

He stood back and waited a few seconds and then knocked again, this time more firmly.

"Yeah, come in," was the response from the other side of the door.

He entered the large, sparsely decorated room, with a bookcase running along one side of it and a couple of paintings on the other wall - obviously laid out as someone's office or study.

He immediately made eye contact with the man at the other end of it, who was sitting behind a sizable wooden desk, which was completely clear, apart from an A4 size red leather logbook in the centre.

He was dressed in a well-cut black suit with a matching claret shirt and tie, leaning back in a large black leather chair. John now felt very much underdressed, sporting a scruffy pair of grey combat trousers and a badly wrinkled t-shirt.

As he approached the desk, the man stood up and extended his hand.

"I'm Doug and you must be John."

They shook hands and John nodded his head.

"That's me."

"Take a seat."

John sat down in the seat facing Doug, an expensive looking wooden chair with a padded green leather back. Doug opened the red book and started flicking through the pages.

"So you're a friend of Michael's, is that right?"

"I am indeed, yes."

John was smiling and trying to seem enthusiastic, while Doug remained engrossed in flicking through the red book.

"Thailand wasn't it, you met in Thailand?"

"Yes, we were staying in the same hotel in Thailand, went out drinking and before you know it, we were travelling round Australia together. We were both on our way there to travel for a year and we got on well, so we thought we might as well travel together."

Doug nodded in recognition that John had finished speaking, but at this point, was obviously more concerned with whatever information was contained within the red book.

"Here you are."

Doug looked straight up at John.

"I've found your details."

John certainly wasn't expecting this. He thought Michael had just mentioned his name over the phone. Details, what details?

Doug eased back in his chair again.

"So John, Michael tells me you're a bit of a hard man."

John didn't know what to say, but bowed to his natural cockiness when searching for a reply.

"I have my moments."

"Moments, yes. Michael told me about the moment when you pair ended up fighting with five guys outside a bar in Perth. In his view, you saved both your lives. Two of them had knives didn't they?"

"Yeah, we were lucky not to get hurt."

John wasn't sure where this was going. Why had Michael told him about this?

"Lucky? Michael tells me you floored one with a single punch, one with an elbow, relieved one guy of his knife and stabbed him in the leg with it. Hardly luck."

"Well, it was them or us who were going to get hurt, so it was them. Do you know what I mean?"

These words brought an obvious smile to Doug's face, a smile that told John they were exactly what he wanted to hear. Michael had been cagey about the work he would be doing, but it now seemed clear that it would be utilising his physical capabilities to some extent.

Doug gestured to the large picture frame on the wall to his right. John had not noticed on the way in, but it contained a large black and white photograph of Muhammad Ali shadowboxing underwater.

If John had to name someone as his hero or inspiration, he would have been torn between Bruce Lee and Muhammad Ali. Both of these iconic individuals had had a huge influence on him since childhood.

The fact that he had this famous black and white photograph of Muhammad Ali on the wall of his office impressed John and instantly made him warm to Doug.

"Ali, the best ever. I believe you're into boxing," said Doug.

From a boxing point of view, John's all time favourite fighters were Muhammad Ali and Mike Tyson. John saw no point in bringing Iron Mike into the conversation at this juncture though.

And Doug was absolutely right that John was into boxing. If anything, that was an understatement. He was obsessed with boxing. He loved Thai boxing as well.

"I do boxing and Thai boxing. I used to do judo as well and I try to read up on as many forms of combat technique as I can. It's just something I've always been into, but I haven't really trained properly in ages."

"I train every day. Weights, bag work, sparring - the works. A lot of the lads box, so I'm never stuck for a sparring partner.

You see John, the way I see it, life's too short to waste your time. I love to train, I love to box and so I devote a lot of time to it; to turning myself into something better than what I started with.

That for me is living life. Not for everyone, but for me. Photocopying bits of paper, serving people food or what?"

Doug quickly scanned the page in the red book.

"Selling people bits of cardboard on their doorsteps, or answering phones all day. To me, that's no way to live life. To me, that's a waste of life."

Doug looked him straight in the eye.

"You know what I mean, don't you John?"

John didn't reply, but he knew exactly what Doug meant.

"When you stabbed that guy in the leg, how did you feel about it?"

Doug leaned back in his chair again.

"Fine," was John's casual reply.

"You hurt someone badly and you broke the law and you felt fine?"

"He deserved it. They were looking for a fight, carrying knives, they deserved what they got."

"I agree John, so would anyone with any sense, but in the eyes of the law, you committed a crime. How would you have felt if Michael had gone to the police?"

"I wouldn't have been very happy."

"No, I don't imagine you would. You'd expect loyalty from your friend, as well as common sense. After all, you had to do what you did. Anyone could see that.

And that is all I ask John, loyalty and common sense. An understanding that sometimes things have to be done that may be extreme and could carry a sentence with the law.

But if everyone does what they have to do, stay loyal to each other, keep business matters within the business and use a bit of discretion, then we're all happy and we can all spend our time doing something a little bit more productive than voucher-based sales."

John wasn't really sure what to say, so he just nodded. The seriousness of what he was getting involved in was now hitting home.

"I'm gonna be honest with you here John, we're very selective about who we bring in. We work on recommendation only and Michael recommended you very highly. You seem like the kind of guy we want.

We're a very close-knit unit here; we trust each other with our lives. We're like a family. You've seen the tattoo on Michael's arm?"

"Yeah, he's not shy about showing people."

Doug took off his jacket, hung it carefully over the back of his seat and rolled up his shirtsleeve, revealing a tattoo on his forearm, identical to Michael's. A thick black number one with the words 'all for' and 'for all' circling it.

John had always liked the tattoo, but had never asked Michael about the significance of it, which was now becoming clear.

"It's a symbol of unity and brotherhood. Some of the guys live here, some don't, but we're all available to help each other out whenever necessary, and sometimes it can be really necessary.

Don't get me wrong, we're not the fucking Partridge family or anything. We don't all go on picnics and hold hands. There are personality clashes and some of the guys don't like each other very much - that's inevitable.

We've had times before when people have fucked each other off and they'll put gloves on and go hell for leather in the ring, but afterwards they shake hands and move on. We don't all have to be best mates, but when it comes down to it, you've got to be prepared to go the extra mile for each other."

This was a lot to take in, although John wasn't hearing anything he didn't want to hear, but he liked to deal in specifics. By no means did he feel bound by morality to avoid doing something that required him to bend the law, nor did he mind making use of his fighting skills, but now he wanted to know everything.

He sat forward in his chair, leaning his forearms on Doug's desk.

"Doug, your philosophies on life are pretty close to mine and I like the idea of training every day instead of wasting my time - I love that idea, actually. But my bank balance is minus three hundred pounds and I've got a two thousand pound personal loan to pay back, not to mention student loans. So, to put it bluntly, what exactly do you want me to do and how much are you going to pay me?"

Doug slowly raised himself up out of his chair and paced around the desk, holding his forefinger to his mouth, until he was right beside John. He took his finger away from his mouth and turned to him.

"Direct and to the point. I like that John, I like it. Come with me."

He started making his way to the door and John quickly got up and followed him, still keen to have his question answered.

Chapter Three

The way Doug talked about his lifestyle really hit home for John. Why waste yourself doing something pointless, when you can spend your life being productive in your own eyes?

He had quite enjoyed his first couple of weeks on the dole after the call centre, until his savings ran out and he couldn't afford the gym every day.

They were walking at quite a relaxed rate through the corridors, as Doug was setting the pace. John was still in awe of how impressive the house was.

"This place is amazing. It really is massive."

"It's not bad," was the coolly understated response.

"How much would a place like this run you, just in case I decide to get one?" John laughed.

"Seven figures. They're not cheap. You never know though, if you play your cards right, you might be able to afford one by the time you're my age."

His age! John was guessing he was in his early thirties at the oldest and he was usually pretty good with ages. The most there was between them was maybe ten years.

"How did you pay for it anyway?"

"Cash."

They came to the top of a winding metal staircase, looking slightly out of place amidst the general old world, varnished wood look of the house interior, and began to make their way down it. Doug turned to him as they walked.

"Michael tells me you're a pretty good shot."

"Yeah, it seems so. I never knew I was, until we went to that shooting range in Cairns and I couldn't stop hitting the centre of the target. Even with the Magnum .44, and that is a hard gun to shoot. I mean, I don't know if you've ever fired one, but it's like a fucking cannon. It just seemed really easy to me. Aim and shoot."

"You are from Belfast; are you sure that was your first time holding a gun?"

John had lost count of the number of references to guns and bombs he had heard from people, when he told them where he was from, in the course of the trip around Australia. It was a lot though.

"I used to have an air pistol when I was a teenager, maybe that helped. Same sort of thing, just less of a kickback."

"An air pistol," Doug repeated, grinning.

At the bottom of the staircase there was a soundproof door, directly in front of them. As Doug pulled the door open, John quickly realised what they were entering. It was a shooting range.

And this was not just a scaled down, home model. This one was bigger than the one he had paid to use in Australia. The one in Australia could have three people shooting at once, but this one could have about fifteen.

Sanjay was at the far end, loading what looked like a .45 automatic.

"Alright Sanjay, John's about to make you look bad here mate!"

Doug turned to John.

"Sanjay's not much of a shot you see. You should give him some pointers."

Sanjay smirked slightly, by no means a full smile, before giving his response.

"Fuck off."

He stepped up to the counter in position to shoot, set down his gun and put on a set of blue industrial earplugs, which reminded John of nineteen-seventies music headphones. Then he took a target sheet, clipped it up in front of him and held down the button to send it sliding back to the end of the gallery. Doug and John stood a few feet back from him and put on earplugs.

Sanjay picked up the .45 again, cocked it and took aim, clasping it tightly with a standard two-handed grip. He fired eight shots in succession, with a few seconds pause between each one.

As the target slid back up along the ceiling, John knew he could do better. Sanjay wasn't bad - one in the centre, the rest not ridiculously far away - but not quite up to what John knew he was capable of.

Doug took his earplugs off and signalled John to do the same.

"Sanjay likes to use a .45, but I think that's all bravado. These high calibre weapons, I mean it's not like we're in fucking Sierra Leone or anything. Myself, I like to use a .22 automatic. It's a nice weight, not too much kickback, feels nice in your hand and if you shoot to kill, you'll kill what you shoot. What's your preference John?"

John was tempted to try the .45 automatic that Sanjay had used, but decided it was best to be shrewd and continue his rapport building with Doug by opting for a .22.

"I fired a .38 and a .44 Magnum in Cairns. I preferred the .38, but I'll try a .22."

There was a long metal cabinet along the back of the room with handguns just lined up on the top shelf. Then below were piles of ammo.

Doug reached on to the top shelf and produced a .22, sliding an already loaded magazine into it. He handed it to John.

"Take off the safety and you're ready to go."

They both put their earplugs back on and John stepped up to start shooting. He clipped a target sheet of his own above his head and held in the button, sliding it to the back.

As soon as it was in position, he took aim, holding the pistol with a two-hand grip, and fired seven shots in quick succession, each one hitting the target in the centre circle. After pausing for a few seconds, he lowered the gun and held it pointing at the ground in his right hand.

He then turned to the two onlookers to see if his shooting met with their approval. Doug was puzzled as to why he hadn't fired all of the bullets.

John spun back around to face the target, quickly raising the pistol back up in his right hand, leaving his left hand by his side and fired the last three shots.

As the target sheet slid back towards him, he didn't see anything he didn't already know. All ten shots dead centre. The three of them took off their earplugs and set them on top of the cabinet.

Doug was impressed.

"You're a cocky bastard and a good shot John, two qualities I admire in a man. What do you reckon Sanjay?"

"That was good shooting."

John was very pleased with himself. He had been confident stepping up to shoot, although he hadn't been sure that he could match the accuracy of his performance in Cairns. Once again, he had shown himself to be a natural marksman.

After growing up on a diet of action movies, from James Bond as a child to John Woo as a teenager, he had always had an immature fondness for guns. And firing them in real life had been no let down either. He felt very much at home with a gun in his hand.

"How did you find the .22?"

"Nice. It was easy to shoot and I had total control over it, even with one hand. Better than the .38 in Australia."

"A man after my own heart."

Sanjay began reloading his .45, while Doug patted John on the back.

"Let's head back up to the office and leave Sanjay to get some practice in."

Sanjay glanced up at him with a look of disapproval and then went back to loading his gun. They went out through the soundproof door and headed back the way they came, up the winding metal staircase.

Chapter Four

As they both took their seats again at either side of the table, John was keen to know the details of what was required of him. He had already decided that he liked Doug and that he liked the lifestyle Doug was presenting, but what did he have to do?

"Well John, the time has come. You wanted to know about work and money; well it's simple. You saw the guns downstairs; you fired off some rounds and enjoyed yourself. Those are illegal weapons; we just broke the law, but I must say, I'm not exactly overcome with guilt. What about you?"

John shook his head.

"Of course not. We like shooting guns, so we got some guns and fired them. No harm done. You see if you make your own rules in life, rather than going by those laid down by others, you find that it becomes a lot more enjoyable.

In general, you think of the law being enforced by the police. For the most part though, it's not, it's enforced by people on themselves, because they're afraid of what'll happen if they get caught. So the answer to your question is, if you want to live life exactly the way you want to, rather than following convention, then you've got to defy convention to finance that lifestyle.

And you can do it if you want, but you've got to have loyalty. Do you remember the robbery attempt at the Millennium Dome?"

"Yeah, it was all over the news at the time, I remember."

"That's right, but the story did not have a happy ending, because they got caught. It was a good plan and they executed it well, but they got caught because someone grassed."

"It was a shame, they would have gone down in history like the great train robbers. It would have made a great movie."

"Exactly!"

Doug was impressed with John's response.

"But some fucking low life ruined it. That's why we run a tight ship here and we have to trust each other like brothers. It's also why I'm so careful about who I bring in. I don't hire dumb thugs, or anyone I'm not sure about. But clearly you're an intelligent man; you've got a degree don't you?"

"I do, not that it's been much use to me. I'm twenty-three, I graduated two years ago and I've yet to have a decent job."

"Yes, but you had the intelligence to pass the exams and to be honest John, I've got no doubt that you're the kind of guy we like to have here. So..."

Doug reached into his desk drawer and pulled out a plastic bag the size of his hand, tightly packed with white pills and set them in front of him. John knew what they were.

"You take ecstasy, is that right?"

"I've been known to," John replied coyly, "not so much in Australia - coz they're so damned expensive there and we were skint half the time - but in general, it's definitely something I do."

"Well, if you come on board with us, you're going to be selling them. Drugs provide us with our regular weekly income. Ecstasy and to a lesser extent speed and coke. We find it's a low risk, high profit enterprise, with no difficulty getting customers."

John had no problems with this.

"Some of my mates at home deal and I've thought about it myself, but of course the problem in Northern Ireland with dealing is that you run the risk of getting into trouble with the paramilitaries and that's no fun. You'd much rather get into trouble with the police than those boys. At least the police would leave your kneecaps intact."

"So, you're happy with the dealing then?"

"Yeah, no problem. I assume I'll be dealing in Manchester."

"We mostly deal in Manchester and places nearby. A couple of the lads go to Liverpool and a couple go up to Leeds on a Thursday night, if they need extra cash, but I like to keep everyone close by, so if anything goes wrong, or there's a bit of trouble, we can all get there quickly. Plus, we have a reputation locally, so people generally don't tend to fuck with us when they see the tattoo.

Of course, we get involved in territorial disputes occasionally, but as long as you show that you're willing to take it further than them, they'll tend to back off, whoever they may be. Besides, we control the dealing in enough clubs now that there's rarely any trouble.

If you'd come to me a year ago - when Michael was last here - this work was a lot more hazardous, but not now."

"That's good to hear, but a bit of trouble doesn't really bother me anyway."

"I like that attitude John. Sometimes we have to take things to the extreme, take them to their logical conclusion to overcome obstacles, but I think you'll handle it fine."

John was confident he would.

"Occasionally we do other bigger jobs, but not that often. When we do - if you're one of the ones chosen to be involved - it means a big payday. Our bread and butter are the drugs though."

"So, when do you want me to start?"

"Straight to the point again. Okay, well you can take this bag of two hundred and start tonight. Bring me back a grand and keep the rest. You know the score, a tenner a pop. You can vary that at your own discretion, but try to keep the price high, as you want as much cash for yourself as possible."

John reached on to the desk and picked up the pills, certainly the most ecstasy he had ever held in his hand at once.

"So, where do I go to spread these around?"

"I think we'll start you off in a little drum n' bass club called The Doom Room."

"Sounds friendly."

Doug laughed.

"You'll love it. There'll be no shortage of demand in there. We'll keep it simple for you, dealing pills only tonight. You'll be on your own, so get them sold and get out.

Some of the lads like to take a couple while they're on the job, but I'd advise that if you're up for dropping, wait till after you're done. People will be partying here all night after they get back.

When you're carrying the kind of money you will be, it's best to play it safe, so like I said, I'd get out once you're sold out and keep your head together till you're back here.

Any questions?"

"Is the tattoo compulsory?"

"No, it's up to you if you want it done."

"How many of the lads have it done?"

"All."

"I see. Looks like I could be getting a tattoo then."

"One step at a time, let's see how you go circulating these pills and we'll worry about the tattoo later. Now, I'm guessing you'll want to talk to Michael, so I'll show you to the main hall; that's where he'll be. Oh, and if you need somewhere to stay, you can have a room here for as long as you like. As I said, some of the lads live here anyway."

And that was it, organised with a place to stay, a potentially good income and in England rather than Belfast. He had really been sold on the idea of the lifestyle. Spending his time doing things he enjoyed, with a minimum of time spent earning money.

It's probably what most people ideally wanted, he thought, and now it seemed like he could have it.

Chapter Five

As he walked in, he marvelled at the size of the main hall. It was a huge room with a wooden balcony running right round above it, matching the flooring and wood panelled walls.

There was a huge widescreen TV with a PlayStation 2 hooked up to it, as well as a DVD player and a VCR. The TV was switched on with an unwatched demo of a soccer game running on it from the PlayStation 2.

There were black leather sofas in front of it, as well as other comfortable and expensive looking furniture scattered around the hall. There were even a couple of La-Z-Boy reclining chairs at the other end, by the stereo and pool tables.

No shocks for John; Michael was playing pool with someone. Michael loved pool, but much to his disgust, John wasn't much good at it and found it pretty tedious. Thus, all around Australia, every time he found a willing volunteer, he was lost to the pool table until nobody else wanted to play.

Michael was leaning over to take a shot, but saw John walking towards him and stood up to greet him, putting his shot on hold - temporarily.

"Here's Johnny!" was his loud greeting, in his traditionally poor Jack Nicholson voice.

He then dropped the Jack Nicholson impersonation and continued in his usual speaking voice.

"Come on up here and we'll teach you how to play pool. This is Ben, by the way."

Ben nodded in John's direction, John reciprocating. John hated formal introductions, so the nod was fine with him.

"Well John, I'd like to say I've heard a lot about you, but Michael only mentioned you for the first time five minutes ago."

"Hey come on, since I've known John I've only spoken to you what...five, six times on the phone?" Michael laughingly interrupted.

He was keen to make a joke out of it, although it was true that he hadn't mentioned John to Ben up until now.

"What can I say? There was always something more important to talk about."

Now that Michael had made his tongue in cheek excuses, Ben spoke up again, wanting to get to know John and also eager to confirm his belief that John was now on his way to being part of The Brotherhood.

"So, Michael tells me you could be working with us."

John slumped back into one of the La-Z-Boys, spun it to face the two pool enthusiasts and then reclined it, so that his legs were in the air and his head leaning back at a forty-five degree angle.

"Come on then Johnny, spill the beans," Michael added.

He was keen to hear how things had gone, although he was lining up his shot on the pool table again as he spoke.

"How did things go with Monsieur Griffith? Did he love you or what?"

John removed the bag of pills from his pocket and dropped them on his stomach.

"Everybody loves me Michael, you should know that by now," was John's happy reply.

John smiled and began fidgeting with the bag of ecstasy pills.

"I start tonight my friend."

Michael potted his ball before reacting. He walked over to John, leaning his pool cue against the table on his way and offered him his hand. John enthusiastically shook it.

"Welcome aboard man. I knew he'd love you. This is good news."

Michael took a step back.

"So, has he told you about the shooting range yet?"

"I've already tested it out and it is very much to my liking. Shot ten rounds from a .22 automatic, dead centre."

"Not just a fluke then, that time in Cairns?"

"I told you Michael, I have a natural gift. There is me and then there's Woody Harrelson; natural born killers," replied John, with a grin of self-satisfaction.

"What about the gym, did he show you the gym?"

John shook his head.

"Oh, you of all people are going to love the gym. Weights machines, free weights, running machines, cross trainers, all kinds of fitness machines, loads of punch bags and best of all, a full size boxing ring."

"This is my kind of place. Doug had mentioned you guys train all the time, but I didn't know the gym was that good. This whole place is fucking amazing and the job itself doesn't sound too taxing."

"Yeah, well Doug keeps us pretty busy sometimes, but it's all good; it's all money. And the thing is, all the shit you've got to do is just no big deal. The first time you're dealing, you're pretty nervous, but after a while, it's a real piece of piss. And you're fucking loaded - "

Michael was about to continue, but John jumped in.

"Hold on a second. While we were travelling, you were just as skint as I was half the time."

Michael held his hands up.

"What can I say, no matter how much I get, I'm no good with money."

John was already well aware of this fact, having often voiced his disapproval of Michael's obsession with all forms of gambling and of his unnecessarily expensive shopping habits. Michael liked his clothes with expensive labels attached.

"I made the mistake of taking a couple of weeks out, to get myself organised to go. Ended up waxing loads of my cash. But you, if you'd been in this line of enterprise for a while before going, you would have been fucking flush for your trip; seriously fucking flush."

"So, you reckon I've landed on my feet then?"

"With my help mate, you have landed in a big pile of money."

If things went well, John knew this would just be the beginning of this line of conversation, with remarks like, "Where would you be if it wasn't for me?" But so far, it did seem that Michael had set him up very well.

"Where's he starting you out?" piped up Ben.

He had remained hovering by the pool table, but was still very much involved in the conversation.

"Oh, it's a drum n' bass club called The Doom Room. Do you know it?"

Ben paused for a second and then nodded.

"Yeah," was all he said.

Michael moved back to the pool table, picking up his cue again, to continue the game.

After an extended silence - when Michael and Ben seemed engrossed in the pool table as Michael prepared to take his shot - John got the impression that the conversation had been abandoned.

"You pair aren't saying much, is there something I should know?"

"You'll do fine John. You've got star quality," was Michael's indirect response.

He seemed like he was being somewhat evasive, as he leaned over the table to take his shot.

"Jim Morrison had star quality and he's dead. Star quality's no good to you when you're dead. Now is there something I should know?"

John was determined to get an answer, but Michael momentarily ignored his continued questioning, in favour of his pool game.

He hit a soft shot for the side pocket, but slightly too soft, the ball stopping dead in front of the pocket, a hair's breadth from going in. Michael groaned and turned his head in disgust, before turning back to face John and give him the answer.

"There is something you should know Johnny. We're a brotherhood here and we're in it together and everything, but at the end of the day, Doug's the man who makes it all happen.

Much as I'm not one for doing what I'm told, he's the boss. He's the most agreeable boss I've ever had, but he's still the boss. Doug says sell - how many pills did he give you?"

"Two hundred."

"Two hundred pills, right, he says sell two hundred pills in The Doom Room and bring him back a grand, then do it and do your best to get a tenner for each one. That's all you need to worry about."

Moments of sincerity from Michael were rare, so when they came, John tended to listen. It was clear that this was a no questions asked situation.

Adopting a similarly sincere tone to that which his friend had used, he responded.

"Michael, I've got to tell you something that only a friend can."

He paused, looking as if he was about to break some disturbing news, before continuing.

"That last shot of yours was the most womanly effort I have ever seen."

Ben burst out laughing, Michael joining in after a second, reluctantly.

For the next couple of hours John stayed in the main hall, watching his old friend and his new acquaintance playing pool and eventually being roped into playing himself. He then got Michael to show him to one of the bedrooms, as the fatigue of over twenty-four hours travelling began to set in.

He felt like he could have slept for about two days, but unfortunately for him, he only had a few hours before he would have to be rudely awoken by the tiresome - and all too familiar - droning of his travel alarm. After all, he had a busy evening ahead.

Chapter Six

John had taken the precaution of securing the bag of pills in his crotch, as his dealer friends in Belfast would do, if they were concerned about getting searched. No bouncer was going to go fishing in his underwear to check for drugs. He had been told it was illegal for them to do so, but even if it wasn't, the thought of a nightclub bouncer with his hand down another man's crotch didn't seem probable.

Anyway, Michael had told him he would never get searched at this place. Apparently it was the type of club where the management expected dealers and drug taking patrons and appreciated that this was the market they were catering for, although didn't get involved in the dealing themselves.

John was not going to take any unnecessary risks though. He felt it would be just his luck to get caught with a load of pills on his first ever night dealing, so in his underwear the pills would stay, until he was safely in the club.

Ben had mentioned that the place was, in his words, 'a bit of a shit hole' and John's first impressions didn't do much to dispel this rumour. For starters, the entrance was down an alley, around the side of a building and to add extra credence to Ben's harsh judgement, the supremely tacky red neon sign had a faulty M, thus welcoming him to 'THE DOO ROOM'.

The bouncer looked pretty standard, shaved head, goatee beard, bomber jacket, a little bit shorter than John, maybe five foot ten, but big with it. Judging by his slight double chin though, John surmised that the size came more from lifting food to his lips, than lifting weights in the gym. Regardless of how he may have looked, he seemed like he'd need a jolt with a cattle prod to wake him into action, should any trouble start.

He was engrossed in the Daily Sport newspaper, as he waved John to go through the door. John felt he could have rolled the pills into the club in a wheelbarrow without being stopped.

At this point, he vowed not to suffer the discomfort and indignity of a crotch-smuggle should he be working in The Doom Room again, as it certainly seemed he had been overly cautious.

He walked down the entrance steps into a fairly dingy hallway, with a doorway straight ahead into the main club area. He could see that it was quite busy and the atmosphere seemed relatively lively for so early in the night. It was barely ten o'clock, but it could have been midnight, judging by the club.

His first stop was the gents toilets, located to his right, along the hallway. There was only one toilet cubicle, but it was vacant and John went straight in, closing the door.

He was disappointed to find the lock seemed to have been long since broken from the door, so he leaned back against it and reached down his jeans to fetch the pills. He then put the bag into the inside pocket of his denim jacket, took a deep breath and a second to quickly psyche himself up.

With an under his breath utterance of the words, "come on," he emerged from the cubicle and marched straight back up the hallway, towards the main part of the club.

This was it, his life of crime and recreation about to officially start. To say he couldn't wait would have been wrong, but he was certainly keen to get this first night over with.

He not only hoped his next time out would see him less anxious, he also hoped that whatever lingering doubts he had about the choices he was making would be dispelled when he was back at Doug's place, partying and counting his night's bounty. After all, he was throwing himself head first into this, not necessarily because he was sure it was what he wanted, more because he was sure of what he didn't want.

Drum n' bass was not John's favourite genre of music. When he was clubbing, his music of choice would have been techno, or failing that, some funky house. It wasn't that he disliked drum n' bass, more that he wasn't a great dancer and drum n' bass required more of an effort to dance to.

With techno or house, he could just descend into a monotonous dance floor march on the spot, in time with the beat, whereas drum n' bass required bouncing around and a general ability to dance fairly well. This was of little consequence, however, as he was not there to dance.

The main dance floor area was very dark. Obviously nightclubs in general tend to be dimly lit, but even for a nightclub this place was dark. It was clearly not a club for the well-dressed poser.

The clientele in this type of venue were there for the music and the drugs, plain and simple. The place was open until four a.m. on a Friday night and the bar closed at one a.m. There was little danger of a last minute rush for the bar at twelve fifty-five either, unless it was for bottles of water.

John had only just arrived and he was feeling warm in his jacket. This place was hot, heated up by sweaty revellers. No big air-conditioning bills at The Doom Room, he thought.

John ordered himself a bottle of water from the bar and then turned to face the dance floor, quickly scanning the area. He was taking Michael's advice and looking for the person most blatantly under the influence of drugs.

Michael's theory was that if you found the person who was most obviously on drugs - to the extent that everybody knew it - you should approach them and ask if they need any more. The likelihood being that, despite the fact that they may already have had enough pills to keep them dancing until Monday morning, they would still say yes, because in their state, the suggestion of more drugs would naturally appeal to them.

If, however, they had run out of money, or just didn't want any more, that was fine too. All that you needed to do was take up a strategic position near this party person and watch as people approach them, trying to find drugs.

As they were on pills and keen to be helpful, they would point them in your direction; you would fulfil their needs, count your cash and go home happy - easy, according to Michael.

Michael had a whole host of theories on every aspect of life, which John often found somewhat lacking. Ben had backed this one up though and besides, it seemed logical.

It took John all of ten seconds to find his man. He was a skinny white guy with a ponytail, maybe eighteen years old, sporting a 2pac t-shirt.

The dance floor was already busy, but this guy had managed to secure himself an unusually generous space in which to express himself. This was no doubt due to his extremely energetic and slightly over the top brand of dancing and the fact that it was a little early in the evening to look like such a sweaty, face-chewing mess.

John wasted no time in crossing the room to meet his new friend. A firm tap on the shoulder and he had the guy's attention, as much as that was possible.

"Are you lookin' for any pills?" he screamed in the guy's ear.

The guy nodded enthusiastically and gave a thumbs up, indicating that yes, he really did.

John quickly ushered him over to a vacant table in the corner of the room, opposite the bar. It was a discreet spot to do business, which John had already decided to be the place where he would spend the majority of his night.

By the time they reached the table, the guy had already organised two extremely wrinkled ten pound notes, which he handed to John, holding up two fingers, indicating what he wanted. John slipped the two pills into his hand, before shouting a request into his ear.

"If anyone needs any pills, tell them to come over here!"

The high level of the music made it difficult to talk, but the guy understood and gave him a pat on the back, before heading back for some more dancing. And so his work was done.

No sales pitch, no objection handling, he just sat back, took a swig of his bottled water and waited for them to come. And come they did.

The word did not take long to spread and within an hour and a half, the majority of his pills were gone. At this point, he decided a trip to the toilets was in order, to take stock of how many he had left and secure the large pile of cash in his jacket pocket down into his boots, tucked into his socks, for safer keeping.

The hallway and the main area of the toilets were busy with people, enthused in chemical-driven conversation. Fortunately for John though, the solitary toilet cubicle was vacant and once again he leaned his back against the door for security.

He pulled out the plastic bag from the inside pocket of his jacket, to inspect the contents, roughly estimating that there were around forty pills remaining. The inside of the bag was now lined with white powder from the pills and he wasn't going to empty out the contents in a toilet cubicle, just to get an exact number.

He did take out two pills though and tucked them into the small pocket of his jeans. Usually he referred to it as the condom pocket - as that's what he most often used it for - but he wasn't sure of its specific purpose.

Tonight, he would use this small pocket to preserve himself some drugs for the after party - in case he sold them by mistake - although he was fairly confident that just licking all the powder from the inside of the bag would be enough to get him in party mood. Nevertheless, better over-prepared than under-prepared, he thought.

Placing the pill bag back into his right inside pocket, he then reached into his other inside pocket, where he had been storing his cash. He pulled out a fistful of notes, which had just been crammed on top of each other, and tucked them into his sock, inside his right boot.

Then he removed the remainder and tucked them into his left boot. He kept out a couple of twenty pound notes, which he secured in his top pocket, in case he had to get a taxi later in the night.

There was no doubt he was happy with himself. Another twenty minutes or so and he'd be sold out and ready to party, the best part of a thousand pounds better off.

This meant that he would soon be leaving The Doom Room with an amount of cash in his pocket that was over a month's pay in any job he'd done in the past and all he'd had to do was sit back and let people give him the money.

Chapter Seven

He stood up, leaning his weight off the door, turned and opened it, all set to get the 'work' section of his evening over as quickly as possible. The scene that greeted him upon leaving the cubicle was very different to the one that he had witnessed on the way in.

He hadn't heard anything, due to the loud volume of the drum n' bass music vibrating through the walls, but the host of jabbering clubbers had vacated the toilets. In their place were three young guys - who looked like they were of Indian or Pakistani descent - standing by the door, which seemed to have been locked.

They were all of medium height, the two leaning back against the door frame looked to John like they were only about nineteen or twenty and fairly skinny, but hard. The one who was taking the foreground, and who seemed to be the chief instigator of whatever was about to happen, looked older - about twenty-five - and was stockier than his cohorts. He was wearing a hooded top with the hood up and had a look on his face that gave John the impression this was to be more than a friendly chat.

It took John only a few seconds to assess the situation and realise what was going on. He had been involved in his fair share of bar fights, beatings and general violent behaviour in his time and knew these guys were planning to beat him up and scare him.

Hence they had cleared the toilets and locked the door, rather than just waiting for him outside the club later in the night. These guys wanted him to know straight away that everyone in those toilets was scared enough of them to leave the room, without question, on their say so and therefore he should be scared too.

John wasn't overly frightened though. Certainly he was shocked at the situation in which he found himself, but by no means was he really afraid.

He would have been more than happy to fight with any one of them, without much, if any, fear of defeat or significant injury. Despite the fact that they looked reasonably hard, they just weren't that big physically, although there were three of them and John was reckoning there to be a fair chance they might have weapons. To what extent they were capable of using any weapons or indeed their bodies to inflict harm was another matter.

So, even though he was certainly not at his ease, or as calm as he was going to give them the impression he was, he was not scared.

"I hear you're the man to see about getting pills," were the first words from the stockier man.

John gave his reply to this stockier man - who seemed like the leader - casually, showing no fear whatsoever.

"Yeah actually. Why, are you lookin' to buy some?"

There was no point in trying to hide or deny what he was doing there, as they were obviously well aware.

The stockier man reached into the pocket of his baggy, combat style trousers and produced a plastic bank bag with perhaps a hundred pills in it and set it on the sink unit.

"Nah mate, I've got my own pills - in fact, I've got enough for everyone."

He paused and turned to one of his partners in crime behind him and held out his hand. A metal hammer was produced from inside the guy's jacket and handed to him.

John was ready for what was coming.

"So, what I wanna know," said the guy, turning around to face John again, "is how come, if I've got enough pills for everyone in here, like I always fuckin' do, you are walkin' around here fuckin' dealing? You're fuckin' dead you cunt!"

With that, he charged at John, swinging back the hammer, ready to strike a vicious blow. Before he had a chance to make contact though, John, rather than retreating as the guy expected, leapt forward and struck him in the throat with the outside ridge of his right hand.

As the guy dropped to the ground holding his throat and gagging, John grabbed the hammer from his now loose grasp, just in time to strike the first of his two-man back up team squarely in the nose with it. There was an explosion of blood as his nose shattered, spattering John's face and clothes.

Like his friend, he fell to the ground, leaving the one remaining attacker to be beaten down with three hammer strikes to the side of the head, collapsing back on to the grubby tiled floor.

The stockier one was still gagging from the hard hit to the throat he had received, when John stomped his boot down on his face and followed it with a hammer blow. He then knelt down beside him, setting the hammer down on the ground.

"Well mate, I'm still alive. Now what have you got for me?"

John searched the pockets of his hooded top, finding one ten pound note and a lighter, but he had more success in the large pocket on the leg of his combat trousers, pulling out a wad of notes, maybe three or four hundred pounds.

Finding nothing in the other pockets, he moved to the guy's trainers. They came off easily, as the laces weren't tied, revealing a couple of hundred pounds shoved in each.

"Great minds think alike," John said laughingly.

He stuffed the money into the empty inside pocket of his jacket and moved to the other two, quickly searching them as well. Between their pockets and trainers, he got an extra few hundred pounds, which he added to the cash pile in his jacket pocket.

He then stood up, picking up the hammer and walked towards the door, dropping the bloodied weapon into the swing top bin against the wall.

As he reached to unlock the door and make his exit, he paused, smiled to himself and turned back again, facing the three injured men on the ground.

"You nearly got off easy there lads. Not quite, but you nearly did."

He made his way back across the room, until he was nearly standing over them.

"You seem like a resourceful bunch, I'm sure you know where to get more of these," were his sarcastic words to them.

He picked up the bag of pills that had been placed on the sink unit and put them into the inside pocket of his jacket, on top of the money he had taken from the members of this beaten drug gang.

Then, he said goodbye to these rival drug dealers.

"Maybe see you next week boys."

He turned, walked back across the room, unlocked the door and swiftly made his way out of the club.

As he walked away quickly up the street, he was amazed at how euphoric he felt. Things had certainly not gone to plan and this incident did not inspire him with confidence about future work for Doug, yet for once he was airing on the side of optimism.

He had survived an armed attack by three would-be gangsters and sustained no injuries at all. He also had around two and a half thousand pounds in his pocket and boots, as well as almost as many pills as he'd started with and he'd managed to walk out the front door, past the bouncer, without the blood on his clothes and face being noticed.

This was because the bouncer had been engrossed in conversation with a scantily clad young female clubber, but nevertheless, a stroke of luck.

He wiped his face with tissues, until there didn't seem to be any more blood. To be sure though, he stopped and looked at himself in the glass of a phone box.

The blood was gone and he let out a sigh. Staring at his reflection, looking into his own eyes, he knew this was it. This was the beginning of a new beginning.

And despite lingering doubts and uncertainty about what lay ahead, he couldn't help but continue to feel elated.

NEIL WALKER

Chapter Eight

There was an enormous sense of satisfaction for him, as Sanjay sank the black to win the game. Mainly because Doug had just beaten him three times in a row and also because it was his third attempt to pot it.

They often took the opportunity to use one of the pool tables in the main hall of Nathan House in private, while the other members of The Brotherhood were out selling drugs.

"Oh, I knew if I played you enough times you'd win one eventually," Doug laughed.

Generally he didn't like to lose at all - at anything - but after beating Sanjay three times, it didn't bother him to concede victory.

"Just warming up, this is the start of a come back."

Sanjay began piling the balls on to the table for the next game.

"What do you reckon to the new guy?" asked Doug, chalking his cue.

Sanjay lifted the triangle on to the table and paused for a second.

"A bit cocky," was his considered reply, "but he's good with a gun."

"The best I've seen and according to him, that was only his second time shooting, except for an air pistol."

"An air pistol," Sanjay repeated, chuckling to himself and shaking his head in disbelief.

Doug picked up his glass of gin and tonic and took a sip.

"I think he's got what it takes, as long as a bit cocky doesn't turn into too cocky."

"What's his surname?"

"Kennedy."

"Is that an Irish name?"

Doug paused before replying.

"Yeah, I think so."

"If it's Irish, shouldn't it be like O'Kennedy or something?"

"All of their names don't start with O. Besides, he's Northern Ireland. I think that's slightly different."

"Why, what's the difference?" queried Sanjay.

"I'm not sure to be honest mate. It seems like the people in Ireland are friendly, but the people in Northern Ireland seem to also really like shooting each other."

"True, they do seem to like shooting each other. Fuck knows what this guy John has been into in the past. Air pistol my arse."

Doug smiled and chalked his cue a little more.

"If he makes it back in one piece tonight, I think we should swear him in straight off."

"That's a bit quick isn't it?"

Doug placed the white in position and leaned forward to break.

"If he makes it back in one piece, he probably deserves it. It was a pretty harsh thing to do to someone on their first night out, but I wanted to see if he's as hard as Michael reckons he is."

Doug broke well, scattering the balls around the table and potting one.

"Look out Sanjay, that's a sign of things to come."

"We'd better hope he's hard, coz we wanna send these boys the right sort of message; let them know they'll soon be out of business."

Doug smiled, scanning the table to decide his next shot.

"We're fine either way. If he does well, they'll soon know John is one of us. If he fucks up, he doesn't have his tattoo yet, they won't make the connection and we'll start again next week - no problem.

You can go down there yourself if you want, take a couple of the boys with you and hospitalise them. One way or another, that club is going to be ours within a month. It's a win-win scenario."

Sanjay nodded, appreciating the logic of what Doug was saying and also indicating that he would be happy to take charge of The Doom Room situation the following week, if necessary.

Doug took his next shot, softly potting a second ball. Sanjay had lost interest in the game though, wishing to continue the conversation about John, as he really did feel it was very soon to swear him in, even if he did survive the gauntlet of The Doom Room.

"Are we sure we can trust him?"

"As sure as we can be, yes. I trust Michael one hundred and ten per cent, which is why it didn't bother me him going off for a year. I knew he'd keep his mouth shut and he'd be back working for us as soon as he returned.

I've been proved right too. He's working tonight, even though he just got off a twenty-four hour flight this morning and I'm sure he's kept his mouth shut.

I mean John's his newfound best mate. They've been living in each other's pockets for a year and all the stuff I was telling John today, I could tell it was all new to him.

So, like I say, I trust Michael one hundred and ten per cent and Michael says this guy is as trustworthy as they come, so that's good enough for me. Michael wouldn't jeopardise our organisation any more than we would and he knows this guy inside out."

Sanjay was in total agreement about Michael, but was still wary of swearing John in so soon. He couldn't help it; he just didn't feel at ease with new members, until he'd seen enough for himself to convince him they were dependable.

He wasn't going to argue the point too much, however, as like Doug, he would be very impressed if John made it back in one piece from The Doom Room.

NEIL WALKER

Chapter Nine

Allowing the taxi to drive away first, John pressed the buzzer and faced the security camera. He had found the taxi to be extremely expensive, although he had come a fair distance and it seemed ridiculous to argue over a taxi fare with the amount of cash he had just made.

Generally, he was told he would have no problem getting a lift from one of the others, but it would have been too early to call anyone for a lift home at this time. They would mostly have still been working.

The metal gates slowly swung open in front of him and he made his way up the driveway on foot.

The previous fifteen hours had been quite surreal and there was a lot for John to take on board, not least that this huge palatial house was where he now lived; free of charge, for as long as he wanted. He even had a key for the door at the side of the building, the door that had no doubt been the servants' entrance at some point in the existence of the house.

As he entered, he could hear music booming from the main hall. A pounding acid techno track, very much to John's liking, which boded well for the night ahead.

His fears that he was back a little early for the festivities to be under way were confirmed when he walked into the main hall, to find it practically deserted.

It was quite dimly lit, but he could see that someone had set up decks in front of the stereo and was standing behind them, lighting up a cigarette. To the left of the decks, there were two guys sitting in the La-Z-Boys, drinking cans of beer, with a box of them at their sides, between the chairs.

John had not had the opportunity to meet any of the others through the day, but he saw no point in being shy. He walked straight across the hall and in behind the decks, pointing at the metal box of records at the guy's feet, indicating that he wanted to look at them. The guy held out his hand, gesturing for him to go ahead.

He knelt down and started flicking through them, although few of them rang any bells for him. Techno and dance music in general was something that John enjoyed when he was out clubbing, but he rarely bought anything, apart from the odd compilation CD.

John had been told that techno and house music had been designed for the enjoyment of people who were under the influence of ecstasy; that the drugs came first and then the music followed.

This made sense to John, as he had never understood the appeal of this kind of music until the night he took his first ecstasy pill. He had thought people who were into dance music just had really awful taste, and would liken their enjoyment of such music to people dancing around a car alarm. Then he dropped a white MDMA pill, embossed with a Mitsubishi logo, in a nightclub in Belfast in the late nineteen-nineties and it all changed.

He hadn't even been sure that he'd come up on his first E, until one of his friends pointed out to him that he was up on top of a speaker, dancing with everything he had to music he had claimed to hate a couple of hours previously.

The ecstasy had explained everything. One chemical experience had made it so clear to him.

After that, he grew to love the rushes that could be had from listening to techno and house music on pills, speed and cocaine. He still didn't see the point of listening to it when you were not partying, however.

For everyday listening he preferred more guitar-orientated music - mostly from the nineteen-sixties and seventies - with Jimi Hendrix and The Doors standing out as his favourite artists.

Despite his relative lack of knowledge of specific techno and house artists, he recognised a Laurent Garnier record, which he really liked, and pulled it out of the box for closer inspection.

The guy knelt down in front of him.

"You like that tune then?"

He spoke loudly, to be heard over the music, though for John the music was relatively quiet compared to the wall-shaking volume at The Doom Room.

"I love Laurent Garnier. I've got the album 'Unreasonable Behaviour' on CD."

"I'll stick this one on next then. I'm Stuart, by the way."

He held out his hand and John shook it.

"John."

"Yeah, you're Michael's mate aren't you, from Australia?"

"Well, I'm not from Australia, but yeah, that's where we met up. We've been travelling together for a year."

"I hear an accent there. Where are you from?"

"Belfast - Northern Ireland."

Stuart gave the familiar look of recognition that John was used to when he said he came from Belfast. He felt the need to add a little bit of clarification, upon seeing this look.

"It's not as bad as you think."

"I'm sure it can't be that bad, but some of the shit you see on the news and in films looks fucking harsh."

John nodded; there was no argument there. Unpleasant and violent things happened in Northern Ireland, that was undeniable, but as far as John was concerned it wasn't anything like the war zone people perceived it to be.

On his travels, he had met people who really did think that the people of Northern Ireland were dodging bullets every day.

"You'll be the first one of us who isn't English."

"So I've been told. Maybe I'll be the pioneer and others will follow in my footsteps," he joked.

"Hold on a second."

Stuart took the Laurent Garnier record and stood up, removing the vinyl from the sleeve. He placed it on the available deck, started it spinning and brought his set of headphones up to his ear.

Holding one of them against his ear with his shoulder, he took about thirty seconds to mix from the record that had been playing, into the one requested by John.

His beat mixing was perfect and John was quite impressed. A few of his friends at home were would-be DJs, but none of them were up to a very high standard. Stuart certainly seemed to be a few steps ahead of them.

His decks were Technics as well, while John's friends were all learning on cheaper models. His experience of DJing was limited and he couldn't really use decks at all, but he knew that any DJ who was any good had a set of Technics.

Stuart knelt down facing him again.

"So mate, how did tonight go for you anyway? Where did he start you?"

"A place called The Doom Room."

Stuart looked visibly shocked.

"The fucking Doom Room! Who did he send you with?"

"Me, myself and I," John casually replied.

He sensed that Stuart was aware of possible dangers there and wanted to create the right first impression, of confidence and lack of fear for his personal safety.

"The Doom Room, on your own, on your first night."

Stuart shook his head.

"They certainly gave you a rough ride. How did it work out?"

John smiled.

"Eventful. Certainly eventful."

"I take it you had a run-in with our young Asian friends?"

John leaned forward, holding out a bloodied piece of his jacket into the light.

"Not mine, by the way," was his only comment.

"That's good to hear. You can tell me about it later, but you should probably go up and see Doug and sort him out. He'll be pretty keen to talk to you. He should be up in the office and if he's not there, Sanjay definitely will be."

"Right then, see you in a bit," said John.

With that, he stood up and headed across the hall towards the doorway he had first entered it through, earlier that day.

Chapter Ten

John was impressed with himself, having remembered the route from the main hall to Doug's office; no mean feat in a house the size of this one, filled with a maze of wood panelled hallways.

He knocked twice, firmly on the office door. Doug shouted through his response.

"Come in John."

He entered, finding Doug behind the desk with a drink in front of him, as well as a large logbook - black this time. Sanjay was facing him in a chair across the table, beside an empty chair, which Doug gestured to him to sit in. John closed the door and took his seat, seeming relaxed.

Both Doug and Sanjay noticed the blood stains on his clothes straight away.

"So, how did your first night go? Sell any pills?" were his opening questions.

"Yeah, sold nearly all of them."

John reached into his pocket, pulling out a bundle of money, which he had counted to be one thousand pounds on the way up to the office, and placed it on the table.

"There's your grand."

Sanjay picked up the money from the table and began counting it.

"I'm a great believer in the honour system, but Sanjay likes to count everyone's money. You know what these Pakistani guys are like when it comes to cash."

Sanjay gave Doug his standard glance of disapproval, groaning his dissatisfaction at the flippant comment, before returning to his money counting.

"So, what did you think of The Doom Room? Was it your type of place?"

"It was alright. Drum n' bass isn't really my favourite type of music; techno's more my kind of thing."

If Doug wanted to beat about the bush, John was more than happy to play along.

Doug leaned back in his chair.

"Any problems?"

"I wouldn't say I had any major problems, no?"

Doug smiled.

"Any run-ins with young Asian dealers?"

"That's right, I almost forgot - "

John reached into his jacket pocket, pulling out a bank bag full of pills. He threw them on to the table in front of Doug.

"They sent you a present."

Doug picked up the bag of pills, examined them for a few seconds and then threw them back to John.

"You earned them, you keep them. You can either sell them or take them in your spare time. How many of them were there?"

"Three."

"I take it that's their blood on your clothes."

"Yep."

"Any injuries for you?"

"Nope."

"That's good. That was a pretty rough first night you just had. Everything will be generally easier from here. You'll very rarely be out on your own again and even if you are, in the clubs we usually deal in, you should never have any confrontations.

We're moving into that club and encouraging those young dealers to move out, so I thought I'd send you in on your own and see how you did. It seems you handled yourself okay. Next week we'll go in there and sweep out the rats."

"So I can keep the pills then?"

"They're yours. As long as you bring me back the money I need from the drugs I give you, I'm a happy man. These pills are your own business, but I'm glad you took them. Now tell me, did you hurt these boys badly?"

"Bloody head injuries, nothing severe," John casually responded, as if bloody head injuries were common everyday occurrences.

Sanjay placed the pile of money back on the table, giving Doug the nod to say that it was all there.

"Okay John, I think that's everything. If you want to head downstairs, you could get started on those pills if you like, or there's plenty of booze in the kitchen. You've returned pretty early, but it won't be too long before everyone starts arriving back. Enjoy the party, you've done well tonight."

"Cheers," John said, as he stood up from the chair and made his way to the door.

Just as he was opening it, Doug called after him.

"John!"

He turned.

"Yeah."

"You did remember to take their money didn't you?"

"Oh yeah. I wouldn't forget a thing like that."

"That's good, that's good," Doug replied, waving him away.

As the door closed after John, Doug turned to Sanjay.

"What did you think of that?"

"He really is a cocky bastard," was Sanjay's response, "but he did well."

"He did very well Sanjay, very well indeed. He handled the situation perfectly and showed a lot of balls. We swear him in tonight."

Chapter Eleven

John was on his fourth bottle of beer and his second half pill, by the time Michael and Ben entered the main hall. He was behind the decks, where he had spent the previous hour or so, talking to Stuart and getting a few DJing pointers.

He had snorted his first half pill - having crumbled it into powder - to make the effects almost instant. Stuart had already taken one and a half, so the conversation had flowed enthusiastically, despite the fact that they had just met.

Michael spotted him straight away and waved him to follow himself and Ben over to the PlayStation 2 area. Michael's second passion - after playing pool - was playing video games. This was a passion that John shared to some extent, so he said a brief goodbye to Stuart.

"Talk to you later man."

He left his newfound friend and headed over to speak to Michael. A fair few people had made it back now and the hall was getting busy, but there were still a couple of free seats facing the TV and PlayStation 2.

John dropped himself into the space beside Michael, at the end of a three-seater sofa. Both Michael and Ben were keen to hear what had happened to him at The Doom Room and wasted no time in getting to the point.

"Good to see you survived John. How'd your night go?" Michael asked him straight away.

Ben leaned over from the far side of the sofa, eager to hear the response.

"Well Michael, I sold most of my pills, got ambushed in the bogs of the club by three armed wankers, took their pills and money and walked away with no harm done to myself, apart from a few nasty blood stains on my clothes. So, all in all, not too bad."

John paused and Michael opened his mouth to speak, but John wasn't finished yet.

"Thanks for the warning, by the way," John added sarcastically.

He would have given Michael a harsher degree of verbal abuse, but the ecstasy had him in too good a mood.

"Hey, I couldn't have told you; that's not the way things work. Doug obviously wanted to test you and I couldn't get involved."

"Yeah, he couldn't have warned you," added Ben, who was very much engrossed in the conversation.

"He wouldn't have had to know," retorted John.

"That's one thing you'll have to learn fast Johnny Boy; everyone trusts everyone here."

"Fair enough Michael, I understand about the trust thing and you're right. It's just a little bit more than I was expecting on my first night."

"At the end of the day, you didn't get hurt, you walked away with a tidy profit and you've made yourself look pretty fucking cool. So, relax John."

Ben got up from the sofa, went over to the TV unit and began looking through the PlayStation games. He had obviously lost interest in the conversation, having heard the details of John's Doom Room experience.

Michael paused for a second, watching him and then spun his head back to face John.

"Anyway, you should be kissing my ass, instead of bending my ear. Because of me, you've got a pile of money and drugs in your pocket, you live in a fucking mansion and you do not have to take your stupid dead-end job in Belfast again. Admit it, you fucking love me."

John tried to repress a smile, but couldn't as it crept across his face.

"Alright, alright. This is a pretty sweet deal, I must say, you've come through for me mate."

Michael patted him on the shoulder, before turning with a start as Ben dropped a joypad in his lap. John looked at the mammoth TV screen to see that the latest edition of Pro Evolution Soccer was in the process of loading, a game that he was quite partial to. He felt sure he'd get plenty of opportunity through the night to show his skills.

Ben sat down on the sofa again and he and Michael were all set to go head to head. John still had one more query on his mind though.

"Here Michael."

Michael leaned his ear in John's direction, eyes still concentrating on the screen, as he selected his team.

"I've been thinking, Doug told me everything today, before we decided I was going to get involved in this. Not only that, I'd been a witness to illegal guns and drugs as well. What if I'd turned round and said no?"

Michael replied, "He'd have killed you," in a very matter of fact way.

"What do you mean he'd have killed me? He wouldn't have actually killed me."

Michael sighed at having to explain himself further and tapped Ben on the arm, gesturing for him to lean towards them.

"What would've happened today if John hadn't wanted to get involved with The Brotherhood when Doug asked him?"

Without a moment's hesitation, Ben gave his reply.

"He would've killed you."

He then leaned back in his seat again facing the television, ready to get the game under way.

"He would've fucking killed me!" John shouted at Michael, not seeing the possibility of him being murdered to be quite so run of the mill as the other two.

Michael paused the game of Pro Evolution Soccer - which had just kicked off - and turned to face John.

"Yes John. That's why you can only get in by recommendation, because once he brings you in and tells you about everything, you can't walk away and not join us. We'd all be in jail in no time if he did that.

So we only recommend people who we think will definitely be up for it. If it turns out they are not and he has to kill them, then it's our fault, because we shouldn't have recommended them unless we were sure they were the right type. With you I had no doubts."

"I'm glad you were so confident," John said.

He was shocked and could not believe that Michael had risked his life like this.

"I needed to be. If you fucked up, I would've had to bury the body and as you know, manual labour isn't my thing."

Comments like this were only adding to John's dismay.

"Has it ever happened before; has he had to kill someone like that before?"

Michael looked down, holding his forehead between his forefinger and thumb, before looking back up at John.

"You risked your life today and it won't be the last time. Yes, it has happened before, although only once that I know of, but it has happened.

We've got something good here and we have got to protect it. Sometimes that means using extreme measures. Get used to it John. This is how it is."

Michael turned his attention back to his game, leaving John - not for the first time that day - pondering the situation in which he found himself. The ecstasy made it hard to think clearly and rationally and the news that he would have been dead and buried if he had decided not to get involved was certainly a shock.

He now knew that he couldn't just walk away if he chose to, but although he was shocked at some of their methods and attitudes, he wanted to be part of it. He had to be. It was too good, too tempting not to draw him to it.

After the dread of going home to work, he now had the comfort of a pocketful of cash, his own room in an English mansion and the knowledge that most of his time could now be spent doing things he enjoyed.

Chapter Twelve

By four a.m. the place was very lively and the party was certainly well under way. Everyone was intoxicated by their drug of choice, whether that was ecstasy, alcohol, cocaine, speed, marijuana or a combination of a few of them.

There were a lot of skunk joints being passed around. Indeed, John had involved himself in a few conversations just to get in line for a smoke on one of them.

As the night had gone on, it had occurred to John that if the main hall had been a nightclub, it would probably have been very popular. Good music, classy surroundings, friendly crowd, absolutely no problems with taking drugs - not to mention the pool tables, PlayStation 2 and even La-Z-Boys to chill out in.

There were five or six guys dancing in front of the decks, which were now being used to play some hard house music. John didn't know the guy who was DJing, as Stuart had handed over the decks about half an hour previously. This guy was good, although not in John's view as good as Stuart.

John noticed Stuart sitting by himself, over at the side of the hall on a small sofa and went over to congratulate him on a fine set and instigate conversation. Stuart saw him coming and took a bottle of beer from the half empty box in front of him, offering it out to John as he approached.

John gladly accepted it and sat down beside him.

"Nice set earlier on man, really good."

"Cheers John, glad you liked it. How did your pills work out for you?"

"Yeah, not bad. I only took one, in two halves, early in the night. Since then, it's just been beers and skunk."

"I've been on the booze for the past couple of hours as well. I don't like to take more than two pills on a Friday. If I do, then working the next night is no fun and usually requires a lot of motivational speed."

Stuart took the last gulp of the beer in his hand, set the bottle on the ground and lifted himself a new one, twisting off the top and taking a swig.

"So, have you met many people yet? Have you had a chance to talk to many of the lads?"

"I've had a few random, pilled up chats, but don't remember any names. Apart from yourself, Michael and Ben, I wouldn't really say I know any of the lads yet."

"Don't worry mate, that'll change fast. Within a week, you'll know most of us. Most of the boys are alright, fairly easygoing, but all party animals. Tonight is just typical of what it's like back here every Friday and Saturday, when everyone gets back.

Some of them won't be going to bed until midday. Personally, I like to get to bed by seven or eight, so I'm not too fucked when I wake up. If I'm not tired, I just neck a couple of jellies or something, but I make sure I get some sleep."

Stuart paused for a second, to re-gather his train of thought.

"Yes, anyway, everyone's fine and we're all really tight, but some people get on better than others. We're all around the same age, which is a big plus point.

I pretty much have no problems with anyone. I'd say maybe one or two of the lads enjoy the violent side of the job a little bit too much and that gets to me at times, but apart from that, there's nothing that really bothers me."

This comment got John's attention and made him feel slightly defensive. He was into his fighting arts and in his own way enjoyed violence to some extent, so would he fall into this category?

"What do you mean?"

"Well, don't get me wrong, I do what I need to do in terms of violence and have no problem with it. If I did, I wouldn't be here. A couple of the lads though - just one or two - can enjoy it a little too much and be a bit sadistic at times.

I'm not bitching about them and I would risk my life for them, for every one of the lads the same, that's just the only criticism I have of anyone."

He stopped speaking for a second, before one more thought occurred to him.

"Oh, apart from Ian. I'd criticise the slightly dodgy house music he plays, whenever he gets behind the decks," he laughed.

"I take it that's not him on the decks now though?"

"No, that's Trev. He's a decent DJ, with a record collection I sometimes envy, I must say."

"So man, I'm still not sure what you mean by sadistic behaviour. What kind of stuff are you talking about?"

"Nah mate, you shouldn't listen to me. I'm half-wankered and you haven't met everyone yet. I don't want to influence you about anyone."

"Come on, I promise you won't influence me. What kind of things do you mean?"

John's curiosity was now aroused and he wanted clarification.

Stuart leaned closer to John and spoke into his ear, although it didn't really seem likely that anyone was going to overhear the conversation.

"Okay, you see the guy by the pool table?"

"The one about to take his shot?"

"No, the one with the baseball cap, talking to the guy taking his shot."

"Right, yes I see him."

"That's Simon. I'm sure you'll like him and he's a pretty decent bloke and everything. Quite funny, but I'd say he takes a little bit too much pleasure in the violent side of his job. Takes things a little further than they need to go at times."

"In what way?"

"Alright, this is probably the best example, or the worst example, depending on your point of view.

About eight or nine months ago, we moved in on a couple of clubs that this one guy had been organising the drugs in for years. I mean this was his bread and butter.

Anyway, it was a standard hostile take over, violent, a bit bloody, but after a few weeks, it seemed to be done and dusted - no problems. Add the clubs to the list and that's it.

Then, about a month or six weeks later, Simon's in one of the clubs - the bigger of the two - on a Saturday night. I think it might have been Ben who was with him, but I can't be sure.

So, they've just got there, haven't even sold a pill yet and in walks this bastard - standing out like a sore thumb, wearing a suit, accompanied by a severely hard looking black guy. He's huge, scars on his face, obviously brought along to scare.

The pair of them sit down at a table, the guy unbuttons his suit jacket and he's got a fucking pistol in his belt. He's come down to reclaim his territory, but he hasn't spotted our lads, coz he doesn't know them and of course, they're not dealing yet, so he can't pick them out.

They obviously hold off on dealing and sit across the club from these boys, keeping an eye on them and phone Doug to tell him what's going on, so he can get people down there.

After about three-quarters of an hour, the big guy gets up and goes to the bog. Simon decides to follow him - not interested in waiting for back up - and leaves whoever he was with watching the Dirty Harry wannabe.

The big bloke is taking a piss, right. In walks Simon, not fazed by the fact that this guy is a lot fucking bigger than him, with an empty beer bottle in one hand and knuckle-dusters on his other.

Before this guy knows what's hit him, he's been clocked round the back of the head with a bottle and he's on his back, on the toilet floor, getting his face mashed with a fistful of metal, still pissing all over himself.

Now Simon doesn't hold back, he gives it loads, pounding this guy, makes a serious mess of his face and beats him unconscious. For me personally, at this point I'd say fair enough; the guy comes down to hurt one of us, he deserves to get a severe kicking. I'd have no problem with that at all."

John nodded his agreement.

"But Simon didn't stop there. He pulls this bloke, dead to the world, into one of the toilet cubicles, takes out his Stanley knife and cuts off his balls. His fucking balls!

So he goes back out into the club and sits down opposite Dirty Harry. Now Harry's got himself a nice cocktail sitting on the table in front of him and before he can even ask him who he is, Simon drops these balls into the drink.

Then, he stands up and screams at him, 'If I see you or your boys down here again, I'll get a fucking round of drinks in!' and then walks off.

Now this boy can't believe what's just happened. He's got a gun in his belt; he doesn't even reach for it to take a shot at Simon. He just sits there for a few seconds and then gets up and leaves. Walks away.

After all, how the hell are you going to react when a person cuts someone's balls off and drops them in your drink? And that, as they say, was that. He never came back, never sent any of his boys down - nothing.

So what Simon did worked and Doug was singing his praises for handling it on his own and doing what it took to get the job done, you know. I have to say, from my point of view it was a bit above and beyond.

I couldn't imagine doing that to someone, even if I absolutely had to. Could you?"

John was quite shocked by the story, particularly as he was in a slightly delicate state mentally, having taken a pill earlier in the evening. He was repulsed by what Simon had done and would have hoped never to have to commit such a vicious act himself, although he chose to play down his revulsion.

He liked to play his cards close to his chest and he had just met Stuart that night. Unlike Stuart, drugs and alcohol didn't loosen his tongue too much.

"I must say, it's not something I would like to have to do."

Stuart had been expecting a bit more of a reaction.

"Too right you wouldn't want to have to do it! I'd say that's a step further than I'd like to go."

Stuart paused for a few seconds and took a couple of swigs from his beer bottle.

"Don't get me wrong though. I like Simon and we are all brothers here. Sometimes he just goes a bit far, you know?"

John nodded, taking a swig from his own beer bottle.

Although the story was a grim one and he would now be slightly wary of Simon, he kept focusing on the good points of his new situation.

Obviously, there were certain gritty elements of this lifestyle he was going to have to deal with. People were going to do unpleasant things, him included.

It was not something he relished or looked forward to but, as Michael had pointed out, he would have to accept and come to terms with the harsh realities of the situation he was in.

NEIL WALKER

Chapter Thirteen

At just after five a.m. Trev had clearly had enough of playing DJ and let his last tune fade out. Despite a few moans and groans, most of them seemed to be ready for something a bit mellower than hard house.

Obviously, Trev wasn't going to walk away and leave the room without music, as this would have been a crime against humanity in everyone's eyes. He quickly reconnected the speakers to the stereo and put some CDs in, to play through unassisted for a few hours.

As Trev walked over to claim his place playing Pro Evolution Soccer, John was delighted to hear the Les Rythmes Digitales album 'Dark Dancer' starting off.

Not only was 'Dark Dancer' perfect, not too lively, not too chilled out music for this point in the night, it was also one of John's favourite albums.

He and Stuart had been engaged in ridiculous dialogue for quite some time. Topics had ranged from whether Iron Maiden would have been a better band if Paul Di'Anno had never left and been replaced by Bruce Dickinson, to whether the Americans would have won the Vietnam War if the A-Team hadn't been imprisoned.

John was quick to convey his enthusiasm for the change in background music.

"Man, I can't believe it! I fucking love this album! I listened to it so much on my way round Australia. It was one of the few CDs I brought with me and I never got sick of it."

Stuart was all set to reciprocate his enthusiasm, but was cut short, as the music stopped dead and all eyes turned to the stereo.

Trev, who had pressed the stop button, was pointing dead ahead at the main entrance to the hall and everyone looked around to see Doug and Sanjay walking slowly in.

From their reactions, John could tell that it was not commonplace for Doug to attend the 'after-work' parties, as they continued across the hall to the pool tables.

Doug then jumped on top of one of them, while Sanjay stood beside it, striking a pose reminiscent of a secret service agent guarding a head of state. It was at this moment that it occurred to John that Sanjay perhaps took himself a little too seriously.

Doug opened out his arms and began to speak loudly, like a ringmaster addressing a circus crowd.

"Alright people, it's good to see you're having a good time and everyone did very well tonight. But as you know, when I feel someone has excelled themselves and really come through, I like to let them know.

Now I'm sure, through word of mouth, everyone has heard about how our new boy John handled himself at The Doom Room. I threw him in at the deep end and he not only did well for himself, he let those boys know their days are numbered in that place.

Hopefully we won't have to hurt them too badly to scare them off permanently next week."

This sent a few laughs and smiles around the room, as it was clearly inevitable that these guys were going to get quite badly hurt.

Doug paused for the laughter before he continued.

"I don't think any of you can say you had quite as hard a first night as John did and considering how well he handled himself, I don't think anyone can have any doubts about his abilities. He's one of us now, so we're going to make it official.

Everyone gather round the pool table, coz we're gonna swear him in. John, that includes you."

John had not been expecting this at all. The only thing he had been anticipating was maybe a couple of sleeping pills - if he could persuade Stuart to donate them - and then bed.

He hadn't even been aware that he needed to be sworn in. Nonetheless, he joined the crowd around the pool table, which was a bit of a crush, as there were a lot of people.

Everyone started placing their hands on top of the hand of the person beside them, so that they all had one hand joining them to the person on their right and one hand joining them to the person on their left. John did likewise with Stuart on his right and Trev on his left.

Even Sanjay was part of the chain, as Doug sat down cross-legged on the pool table facing John and placed his hands, one on top of John's right hand and the other on top of Stuart's left.

"Okay John, including myself and Sanjay, you're gonna be number forty. Over time, we're getting bigger and stronger. All I need you to do is listen to each line I say and then repeat it back to me. What about it John, are you ready to be one of us?"

John replied without hesitation.

"Yeah."

Hearing this, Doug began.

"These are my brothers…"

"These are my brothers…"

"and this is my family."

"and this is my family."

"They can trust me with their lives…"

"They can trust me with their lives…"

"and I can trust them with mine."

"and I can trust them with mine."

"To betray them is to betray myself…"

"To betray them is to betray myself…"

"and put my life in their hands."

"and put my life in their hands."

"I will give everything and more…"

"I will give everything and more…"

"to uplift, protect and bring prosperity to my brothers."

"to uplift, protect and bring prosperity to my brothers."

An enthusiastic round of applause was followed by a flurry of handshakes and pats on the back.

He apparently had thirty-nine new brothers who he had to, 'give everything and more to uplift, protect and bring prosperity to'.

It was a little much for his dazed and delicate brain to take in. He had enjoyed all the friendly attention after being sworn in and he also liked the idea that thirty-nine other people would, 'give everything and more to uplift, protect and bring prosperity to' him.

The fact that he had around one thousand five hundred pounds in his pocket, having arrived in the country without a penny less than twenty-four hours previously, was still giving him a lot of pleasure too.

Still, it was a lot to take in.

NEIL WALKER

Chapter Fourteen

John had often contemplated the idea of getting a tattoo, particularly during his teenage heavy metal phase. He had come very close to getting 'UNSCARRED' tattooed across his stomach - inspired by the singer from Pantera, Phil Anselmo's tattoo - only some persuasive words of wisdom from his mother having talked him out of it.

Of course, he now knew how much he would have regretted getting such a major and ridiculous tattoo done and this had put him off them totally, until now.

He had heard lots of different stories about whether it hurt or not, how much or how little it hurt, people passing out, grown men crying, but he now knew for himself. It did hurt.

It wasn't excruciating and he didn't lose consciousness or weep like a baby, but it hurt a fair bit. He was certainly glad to get back to the house and get the first few tokes on the joint Michael had prepared.

"Come on Johnny Boy, don't hog it," said Michael, growing impatient, as John took his fifth drag.

John passed it over to him, before exhaling.

"Mate I need it. My fucking arm is killing me," he said.

"It's good to get it though, isn't it?" said Ben, who had driven the two of them to and from the tattoo parlour.

"Oh yeah, it's a nice tattoo and now that I've been sworn in, it feels good to have it."

Michael, who was now lying back on the sofa enjoying his joint, added his comments on the matter.

"It must feel good to get it so quickly as well. I can't believe you've been in the country five days and already you're a sworn member, you've got the tattoo and a nice chunk of change in your back pocket."

John's reply was brief and to the point.

"It's all good."

He then reclined in his chair.

Having finished with it for the time being, Michael threw the joint at Ben, causing him to squirm in his chair and quickly retrieve it from between his legs, much to his and John's amusement.

Although this was irritating to Ben, his only retaliation was a single shouted word of abuse.

"Wanker!"

He began smoking the joint, which had managed not to be extinguished during its ordeal.

"I'll tell you what's also nice," said John, "having drugs on tap like this. Pills, coke, weed and speed; at our fingertips whenever we want them. It's a superb situation."

In a reasonably impressive American accent, Michael agreed with him.

"Hell yeah! You're god damn right."

After this, he reverted to his regular English accent to continue giving his thoughts on their current state of affairs.

"Australia was like being in fucking rehab at times. Hardly any gear, pills once in a while, and even then, only one or two. And speed and coke too pricey to contemplate. It's good to be back."

"Are they really hard to come by in Australia then?" asked Ben, setting an example by stepping over to John and handing him the joint.

This was a subject Michael loved to rant about and he did not miss his cue.

"Oh they're not hard to come by…if you're a fucking millionaire. Otherwise, it gets a bit tricky. The prices are so high they're fucking comical.

Fifty dollars for a pill, which is like twenty quid and it broke my heart every time I paid it. A gram of speed, two hundred dollars, which is about seventy-five quid and there's no way I could let myself pay that sort of price; especially as it was probably shit.

Coke is so expensive you couldn't even find it in a club. I think it's reserved for soap stars and politicians.

The drug scene there is a fucking joke and the punchline is that they pay these stupid prices for low quality goods. The real shame is that there are some good clubs there - especially in Sydney - and yet it's a financial nightmare to have a decent night out. Fucking hell!"

Sensing that Michael had momentarily run out of steam, John added his own thoughts.

"If you could get the drugs that we handle into Australia, you could make a fucking fortune. I mean, us as individuals and the organisation would easily quadruple our income."

And back came Michael, as soon as John had finished speaking.

"There you go Ben, now you know what to do. You should take a trip down under with a condom full of drugs up your arse."

This sent the three of them - all looking for an excuse, now that they had some skunk in their systems - into convulsions of laughter. John even forgot the pain of his arm, temporarily.

Chapter Fifteen

Having spent the day sorting out his room and finally unpacking all his stuff, John was not really in the mood for working. In Australia he had grown to despise his rucksack and the tedious ritual of packing and unpacking it, hence his delay in getting fully settled into the house.

He was happy to have got it over with though and after living there for only a week, was still enjoying the awe-inspiring house he was settling into. Indeed, he couldn't believe that only seven of them lived there permanently - as well as Doug and Sanjay of course - when it was so impressive and there were so many rooms.

He was particularly surprised at Michael, who seemed to love being around Nathan House, but was very quick to move into a vacant room in Ben's flat.

Nevertheless, he wasn't in the best of moods, having had a tedious day and the club that he had been sent to with Ian was playing fairly commercial house music, which was doing nothing to improve his disposition. By contrast, house enthusiast and DJ Ian was having a fantastic time, even making the occasional trip to the dance floor in between dealing.

It was just after one of these dance floor outings that the pair met up in the toilets, John just wanting to get his stock sold and get back to the house.

"How are things going? Are you nearly sold out?" he asked Ian, who was a bit of a sweaty mess, having given his all on the dance floor.

"Still a bit to go, but I'm selling well, yeah," was the only slightly satisfactory reply.

A knife cut short the conversation, the blade being held up to Ian's throat by a harsh looking man in a green bomber jacket, quite skinny with a gold hoop earring in one ear, which John was already planning to rip out for him. Ian, seeming very calm, smiled, holding his hand out to John to hold off on the violence.

"I see you cunts are making a bit of money and I've come to get my share," were the menacing words from this knife wielding thirty-something, who sounded to John like he had a Scottish accent, although it was hard to tell.

Looking the man straight in the eye, still seeming very much at his ease for a man on the verge of having his throat cut, Ian spoke a few words to John.

"Show this man your tattoo."

The man turned his head to see John roll up the sleeve of his t-shirt and reveal the freshly done tattoo. The second he saw the Brotherhood tattoo, he pulled the knife away from Ian's throat and retracted the blade.

"Sorry lads. No offence."

He swiftly made his exit from the toilets and the nightclub.

John turned to Ian with a look of confusion on his face.

Ian, totally unfazed by the encounter, cleared things up for him.

"In clubs where we're well established, generally people who try to rip you off just don't realise who you are. It's a quirk of rotating all of us constantly between clubs. Sometimes people just don't know who they're fuckin' with, so you just show them your tattoo and they shit themselves."

"That is unbelievable."

"Believe it mate, believe it. That's what it means to be one of us. Anyone who has any understanding of what that tattoo represents will not dare cross you."

"So, this kind of thing happens all the time then?"

"Not as often as it used to, and it depends what club you're in, but it does happen. And when it does, it is funny as fuck, as you just witnessed."

"It was good, the way that guy totally bottled it and apologised."

"He's probably doing a four minute mile up the street as we speak."

John grinned, amused by the idea of this tough guy sprinting away from the club in fear of a flash of his arm. He was very impressed.

Now he had a tattoo on his arm that had the potential to turn hard men into scared cowards in an instant. The pain most definitely seemed worth it.

As he stepped back out into the club and went back to work, John felt an enormous sense of confidence, bordering on arrogance, fuelled by the idea that who he was and what he was involved in made him a man to be feared. He was now on top form and not even the cheesy house music could bring him down.

Ian's time wasting on the dance floor, which had been getting to him, was now no longer a source of irritation either. After this incident, Ian had gone up in his estimation.

Even though he had known there was a good chance the guy in the toilets just didn't realise who they were, he had remained very calm for a man with a knife at his throat. He had won John's respect and so his questionable taste in music and dance floor antics could now be forgiven.

John was all set for the night ahead, after they had finished dealing, as Michael had built him up for it, saying that it was going to be a really big one. Also, it was Saturday night, so the partying ahead had no serious consequences, no work to worry about and only the prospect of a comedown to hold him back - which it would not.

Chapter Sixteen

John waved his gloved hands to signal that he wanted to stop. As ever, his stamina had been his worst enemy. An entire year without sparring, bag work, or any real serious training had taken its toll. It was going to take a lot longer than two months for him to be in the kind of shape he wanted.

By contrast, Doug looked like he could have continued for a lot longer. He was sweaty and out of breath, but not nearly as exhausted as John, who retired to the corner to let the ropes hold him up. This was the first time the pair had sparred together since John had arrived and Doug had really put him through his paces.

In John, Doug saw someone on the way to being equally as dedicated to training as he was. Perhaps only Sanjay would have had anything close to the same level of dedication, with most of the others training maybe three or four times a week with weights and usually only sparring once.

Doug had an endless appetite for sparring, which never ceased to amaze them all. Sometimes he'd spar with five or six people in one day, each one to the point that they were out on their feet and unable to continue.

John wasn't too hard on himself though, as he felt this level of fitness could be attainable. After all, Doug had been solidly training for years without taking time out, so he knew if he kept training the way he was, over time he'd get better and better and his stamina would gradually improve.

Doug came over and leaned on the ropes beside him, as he pulled off his gloves and picked up his water bottle with a sweaty, cloth wrapped hand, gulping from it like he'd been deprived of fluids for a week. Doug spat out his gum shield so he could speak, although he left his gloves on for some imminent bag work.

"You're getting better John. I've been watching you. Your technique is getting sharper all the time, but we'll have to get your stamina level up."

John pulled the bottle away from his mouth to respond, although he was still in the process of catching his breath.

"I know, I'm still way out of shape. That's what I get for taking a year off training."

"Don't beat yourself up too much. You've come on leaps and bounds since you first got here and you've been training pretty hard. How long is it now, three months?"

"Two."

"It seems longer. You've settled in fast, which is good to see. We've just got to work on your boxing, so I can get a bit of competition," he quipped.

John laughed, his breathing gradually getting back to normal.

Doug continued.

"I've noticed you've been hanging around with Stuart quite a lot. I always see you pair around the place together."

"Yeah, we get on okay, although everyone's been great since I arrived; really friendly. I suppose Stuart and I just spend a lot of time together coz we both live here full time and also coz he's been teaching me to DJ. He reckons it won't be long before I'm good enough to do a set at one of the after parties."

"Another one eh. We seem to have loads of would-be DJs around the place. I must say I wouldn't mind learning to do it myself, if I could find the time."

"I try to work at it every chance I get and then, once I've reached a decent standard, I'm going to focus on learning to drive."

"You can't drive?"

John shook his head.

"To a lot of people, that would be a priority over learning to mix records, but whatever turns you on John, whatever turns you on."

John took off his headgear and Doug leaned his head forward and tapped it with his glove, indicating that he would like John to do the same with his. John obliged and dropped the two headguards down at his feet.

"Cheers," said Doug, before getting back to the main line of questioning he really wanted to explore.

"So, over the past two months, you've been out working in clubs with a lot of the lads and you've got on fine with all of them then?"

John paused for a second and then replied.

"Yeah, pretty much. They've all been fine and the nights have always gone smoothly."

John had got along better with some than others and there were a couple of people who he found a little annoying when paired off with them for a whole night. He hadn't really had any major problems with any of them though, and that's what Doug wanted to know.

John imagined he would like to keep his eye out for any potential grudges or personality clashes, as the success and harmony of the organisation did depend heavily on everyone getting along most of the time. Especially with most of the people involved having no problem with confrontation and the use of violence to solve problems.

In truth though, John had seen the signs of no major personality clashes on the horizon. Even the alleged psycho Simon had been absolutely fine, the night he had been working with him. In fact, John actually found him to be a fairly funny guy, although he remained a little wary of him.

"Tonight, I'm sending you and Stuart out together, to a club called Manhattan Nights. Stuart's worked there plenty of times before, so it should be a walk in the park."

Stuart had told him about the place already. According to him, it was one of the best clubs in Manchester.

"It's probably a bit more up market than anywhere I've sent you before, so dress smartly. They have a no jeans, no trainers policy. You should make a lot of money. There's a big demand for coke there, so you'll make a fortune from that alone, never mind pills and speed.

If you pair just come and see me before you go, I'll get you sorted out and you should have a good one. I'm just gonna finish up with some bag work."

"No problem," said John, climbing out of the ring, all set to get showered and have a nap, before going out on the job.

He was pleased that he was going to be working the Manhattan Nights club, as Stuart had described it as the cream of the crop of Manchester nightclubs, both for glamorous surroundings and for dealing. Also, he was pleased to be working with someone he knew well. He had grown weary of being paired off with people he didn't usually speak to and going through the polite motions of getting better acquainted. Not that he didn't want to be friendly with everyone, but it had become a bit monotonous every Friday and Saturday, going through the same procedure.

The fact that it was a Saturday also had him in a good mood, as it always did, with the novelty of not having to worry about working the next evening having not worn off. He didn't train on Sundays either, both because he was rarely capable of it after Saturday night and because he needed a day for his body to recover from a full week of non-stop weights, fitness and boxing training.

Chapter Seventeen

Manhattan Nights was certainly no let down. It was an impressive looking club, both inside and out - very large and well decorated, populated by smartly dressed men and attractive women.

Doug's promise of a big payday certainly seemed to John as if it was about to come true. Also, Stuart had said that he always found himself a woman in the place, which was another big plus, as far as John was concerned.

He sometimes thought about Lisa. They had known each other and had a kind of on again, off again relationship in Belfast in their late teens. They had kept in touch via email while John was away travelling, although he hadn't emailed her much since his arrival in Manchester.

Ideally, John wanted a real relationship with a woman in his life, and Lisa would have been his number one candidate. This was just impossible with the lifestyle he was currently living though, so he had to content himself with the shallow pleasures of pulling.

He had only pulled a few times since getting to England and only had sex with one young woman. This had most certainly not been through choice; it had just been difficult in his situation.

Even if he wanted to meet a woman when he was in clubs at weekends, his first priority was always selling drugs. Then, if he'd sold out, he wouldn't exactly feel at ease circulating round the club with a pocketful of cash, knowing that half the people would be aware he was dealing and that he was likely to have a lot of money on him.

It was also tricky, as he'd always been paired with a different person he didn't know very well, so he felt obliged not to disappear on them for too long.

And as for sex, John found it was much harder to say 'Can we go back to your place?' than, 'Shall we go back to my place?'

It was totally forbidden to bring strangers back to Nathan House. To do this would obviously be far too risky.

This time, once he and Stuart had made their money, they were on a mutually agreed mission. They were determined to pull women and get some much-needed sex, if possible.

Stuart mimed the act of drinking with his hand and John gave a nod of approval, so they made their way around the dance floor to the bar, keeping their eyes peeled for anyone blatantly on drugs. There were no obvious candidates as yet, but it was only a matter of time.

The club was only half full, if that, and it was only just after ten o'clock. With the club staying open until four in the morning, they were in no hurry, although they wanted to leave themselves at least an hour at the end, to pursue their search for women.

John ordered the drinks, while Stuart leaned back against the bar, surveying the place. As John was paying the barman, Stuart began repeatedly tapping him on the arm.

He waited to get his change, before turning to Stuart, handing him his bottle of beer and asking what he wanted.

"What is it?"

"Don't look now okay, but there's a guy sitting by the wall on my left who should not be here. I really cannot believe this idiot is actually in this club."

John waited a few seconds, and then looked over to see a guy sitting by himself, drinking a pint of Guinness.

"The guy sitting by himself?"

"Yes. Alright, here's what we're gonna do. He obviously hasn't seen me yet, so I'm gonna walk over by the entrance and take a seat. What I want you to do is go up to the person nearest him and ask them if they know where to get any pills. Then go up and ask him. We want him at his ease, so if he says yes, buy one, then come over and meet me by the door."

"I can't believe I'm going to actually buy a pill, when I've got a bag full of the things in my pocket."

"Now make sure you ask someone else near him first. Don't make it look like you've specifically picked him out. Okay?"

"Right. I'll meet you by the door."

He knew all was not well and that this did not bode well for a relaxing evening, full of laughter and fine women. Stuart seemed pretty tense and it was obvious to John that something serious could be about to happen. If this guy did turn out to be dealing, he knew there would be consequences.

As John approached the pasty faced, skinny young guy, he stopped to speak to two attractive young women directly in his line of vision, asking them the all-important question of the night.

"Do you know where to get any pills?"

Not only did the women shake their heads, they gave him a look of derision, as if he had just made a ridiculous and disgusting request. In clubs like this, it was inevitable that there would be a percentage of alcohol purists, who were very much disinterested in the drug use going on around them.

John quickly moved on to his primary target, sitting down beside the guy and once again asking the big question.

"Do you know where to get any pills?"

The guy looked at him smugly, before giving his response.

"How many do you need?"

John held up his forefinger to indicate one, at the same time noticing a severe looking scar on his left cheek, but trying not to stare. He then reached into his pocket for a ten pound note.

Meanwhile, the guy rummaged in his trouser pocket and then produced a clenched fist. He reached it under the table and dropped a pill into John's open hand. John placed a ten pound note into the guy's hand and then walked off across the club to find Stuart.

He was not hard to find. John spotted him at the table closest to the entrance, looking noticeably perturbed.

He sat down beside him, quickly conveying what had happened.

"He's dealing."

"I'm not fucking surprised," Stuart responded, "I just had to be sure, before I call Doug. This guy is in real fucking trouble."

"Why, who is he? What's going on?"

"He's no one. He's just a stupid cunt. He gets cheap pills from somewhere and he deals by himself, for himself and for some reason he's always trying to do it in here. We've caught him twice and he's had two physical warnings. Did you notice the scar on his face?"

"Yeah I did. It was pretty nasty."

"Well that was Simon's handy work, with his trusty Stanley knife. It wasn't improvised; Doug gave the order for him to do it. It was his second warning you see. The first time, I was there and we gave him a very serious kickin'. I couldn't believe he tried to deal here again after that, let alone now, after we cut him.

He must be so fucking stupid. Both times, he was told never to show his face here again and here he is, just asking for it. He's not even that hard. You should have seen him when we beat him up; it was embarrassing how soft he was. Didn't even try to fight back or defend himself. I just can't believe this."

John could sense, by the way Stuart was talking, that he really did wish this wasn't happening. Although he was very capable of the violent side of the job, he certainly in no way enjoyed it; especially in cases like this, where it wasn't even a power struggle. This was just cruelty, to scare someone off trying to deal in a club where they were not wanted.

John didn't relish hurting the guy either, especially now that he'd been told how physically incapable he was, but he rationalised it to himself. If they were to let him get away with it, then word would get around and suddenly everyone would want to move into their clubs.

"I'm going outside to use the mobile and phone Doug," said Stuart, in a resigned tone, as he stood up from the table.

"Stuart!"

John got his attention before he walked away and Stuart leaned down to hear him make an enquiry to satisfy his own curiosity.

"If he hadn't sold me a pill, would you have let him go?"

"I don't know," Stuart replied.

John watched him walk away, as he made his way out of the club to make the phone call.

NEIL WALKER

Chapter Eighteen

Within a few minutes Stuart returned, having received instructions from Doug, and took his seat beside John again, before giving him an update.

"Our relaxing evening is officially ruined. Sanjay is on his way, so he should be here in about forty minutes to collect our friend and us. Doug wants him brought back to the house."

John now knew the guy was dead. There was no way Doug would have wanted him to be taken back to the house, unless he was planning to kill him.

This was all coming thick and fast for John. Within fifteen minutes he'd gone from looking at women and getting ready to sell some pills, to being an accessory to murder.

"What's the plan to get him in the car?"

"Well, we're basically going to have to take our chance when it comes. We watch him and when he goes to the toilets, we go. The fire exit is just up the corridor from the loos, so we grab him, trail him out and just hope there are no witnesses."

"What if there are witnesses?"

"If there are, then we'll have to hope they're more concerned with having a good night and keeping out of trouble than helping this guy. Besides, the most they'll do - if they do anything - is tell the bouncers, who are pretty unlikely to give a shit."

Stuart had obviously moved on from his personal dislike of this side of the job and put his business head on. John was quite impressed, although he was by no means looking forward to executing this - as he saw it - half-baked plan.

"What happens if he goes in the next few minutes and we've got to wait in the alley behind the club with him for half an hour, till Sanjay gets here?"

"After I spoke to Doug, I ran up to the garage and bought a roll of elephant tape. If we have to wait, we'll tape him up and pile a few bags of rubbish on him. Not a problem."

Stuart really had put his business head on. All John could say in response was, "Good thinking. Were you ever in the scouts as a kid?"

Stuart left John's question unanswered. The only thing he was concerned with now was logistics.

"We should move a bit closer to him, before the place fills up more. When we get to a table near him, I'll sit with my back to him, so he doesn't spot me, and you watch him, okay?"

"No problem."

With that, they moved to a table near him; not so near that they caught his attention, but near enough that he couldn't escape theirs.

As it transpired, him going to the toilet too soon didn't prove to be a problem. An hour later they were still watching him, waiting for their chance.

He was now well under way with his night of drug dealing, reaping the dividends that John and Stuart had been expecting. Indeed, for John, watching this guy sell pills was becoming increasingly irritating, while he sat, keeping a low profile, with a pocket full of the things, not to mention coke and speed. He had reached the point where he was all set to do what he had to do and was keen to get it over with.

It had been a tense hour, but the anticipation finally ended as John stood up from his seat and gave Stuart the nod, to let him know the time had come. They quickly made their way towards the toilets, in the hope of catching the guy before he went through the gents door, although not rushing so quickly as to draw people's attention.

Their timing was perfect and they caught up with him just as he was entering the corridor where the gents and ladies toilets were located, with the fire exit door dead ahead of them, at the very end.   Confounding John's Murphy's Law expectation that it would be full of people, the corridor was empty, although they knew they only had a few seconds before someone would inevitably go into or come out of one of the toilets.

They wasted no time, with Stuart grabbing him in a headlock from behind and covering his mouth, while John grabbed his legs.   They charged along the corridor, carrying their squirming victim and slammed through the fire exit door, quickly closing it behind them.

John didn't get a chance to look back and check if anyone had seen them, but it didn't really matter, as they could see Sanjay standing by the car at the bottom of the rusting metal staircase.

It was difficult to keep hold of the guy, as they made their way down.   They were trying not to trip over, while at the same time hurry to the car and hang on to this guy, who was struggling for his life.   It wasn't easy, but they got him to the car, dropping him at Sanjay's feet.

Before the guy could try to stand up, or even really orient himself after being slammed into the concrete, the three began stomping on him, Sanjay taking his head and neck area, John stomping on his torso and Stuart stamping down on his legs. There was no point in trying to tape him up while he was still fighting the inevitable.

He quickly lost consciousness though and they turned him over on his front. Stuart produced the roll of elephant tape he had purchased and taped him up, arms, legs and mouth.

Sanjay opened the boot of the car and the three of them lifted him up from the ground and dropped him in. John was surprised at how awkward and difficult it was to lift the unconscious guy to the car, considering he wasn't exactly huge and they were three strong guys, particularly Sanjay.

Still, within a couple of minutes, they had managed to get him from inside the club to inside the boot of the car, tied up and dead to the world.

It had gone smoothly and as they drove away, John did feel very relieved to have got it over with. However, his thoughts quickly turned to Doug and what he would have in store for this repeat offender.

NEIL WALKER

Chapter Nineteen

They stood at the back of the car and Sanjay turned the key to open the boot. They knew he had come around, as they had heard him banging for the last few minutes of the car journey.

John had opened the side door of the house and they were all set to rush in, although Sanjay hadn't mentioned where exactly Doug wanted him.

As the boot opened before them, he gave his instructions.

"We're taking him to the gym, alright boys."

It seemed to John that Sanjay lived his entire life giving out information on a need-to-know basis. Over the two months he had known him, it had become increasingly irritating. But that was Sanjay.

Getting the guy out of the boot was difficult, particularly for John, who was lumbered with taking hold of his feet. He was doing a fair bit of struggling - as much as was possible, considering his arms and legs were bound. Once they got him out and had a firm grip of him, however, it wasn't too difficult to get him to the gym, although carrying him down the stairs was no mean feat.

They arrived in the gym to find Doug working out on the punch bag, listening to Rage Against The Machine. He noticed them enter and immediately went to the stereo and paused the CD. Usually it would be nearly impossible to hit the button - if he were wearing gloves - but he was training with his hands just strapped, as he occasionally did for bag work.

He turned to the three men, who were eager to relieve themselves of their heavy, struggling load.

"Tape him to the chair," he ordered.

He pointed to one of the metal chairs from the kitchen, which was in an open space, a few feet behind the punch bag.

This was a tough assignment, as in order to tape his arms and legs to the chair, they had to remove the tape currently binding them, to get them separated. The three of them were finding it hard enough to keep control of his wriggling, without freeing his arms and legs.

When they got him to the chair, Sanjay sat on top of him to keep him lodged in a seated position and to limit the movement of his legs, while John and Stuart removed the tape. Despite this, Stuart managed to get a kick in the face, but they quickly got control of his flailing limbs and held them tightly against the legs of the chair.

While Stuart leaned his body weight against the guy's right leg, with one arm wrapped around it, holding it in place, he used his other hand to reach into his pocket to produce his elephant tape. He then taped the leg in place - wrapping the tape around at least eight times, until there was no chance of it getting loose. John then took the tape and did likewise with the other leg.

Sanjay remained sitting on him, holding his upper body in place, while John and Stuart moved on to his arms. They proved easier to control than his legs and were soon taped to the back of the chair. The three of them stepped back, relieved to have finally rid themselves of this troublesome handful.

Now the question of what was going to happen to him again began to cross John's mind. He was under no illusions and knew that whatever happened to this guy would be unpleasant and permanent.

He was not walking out of the building alive. No chance.

"Thank you gentlemen. You've done well, but if you'd like to leave us now, young Peter and I need to talk privately."

It was clearly to be quite a one-sided conversation, as Peter remained gagged with elephant tape. As Sanjay closed the door behind them and they made their way up the hallway, the sound of Rage Against The Machine began once again blaring from the stereo; yet another obstacle to conversation.

As they walked to the main hall, Sanjay explained what would happen next.

"We'll stay together in the hall. I'd say in about half an hour - maybe forty minutes - we'll get a call from Doug."

"What call is this?" asked John, keen to make Sanjay give him the full story.

"The call for us to clean up the mess."

Chapter Twenty

The three of them sat in the main hall, watching the Saturday night movie Lethal Weapon, one of John's favourite action movies, but he couldn't get enthused about it. He just couldn't take his mind off the telephone. It sat on Sanjay's lap, threatening to ring at any second. And then what? Clean up the mess.

What state would this guy, this Peter, be in and what were they to do with him? He could see that Stuart was on edge as well, while Sanjay looked emotionless as always, staring at the screen.

The phone barely got to ring once, Sanjay picking it up straight away, like a reflex action, as soon as it made a sound. He listened for a few seconds and then calmly replied with two words.

"No problem."

He hung up the phone.

"We're on lads," he said to them, setting the phone on the arm of the sofa.

He stood up and made his way back the way they had come, with John and Stuart following, still not saying a word, both dreading what lay ahead.

When they reached the hallway to the gym, they heard Rage Against The Machine stop abruptly in the middle of 'Freedom'. As they approached the gym door, it opened before them, Doug making his way out, very much out of breath.

The wraps on his hands, which were once dirty white cotton, were now red with dripping blood. His upper body was spattered with blood, as were his grey tracksuit bottoms. Indeed, blood and sweat were running down his torso and seeping into the elasticated waistband of his tracksuit bottoms. It dripped from his face and his hair, as if he'd just stepped out of a car wreck.

His mood was in contrast to his appearance though, smiling through his gasps for breath.

"Right then boys, Sanjay will show you what to do. I think I'm in need of a shower."

These were the only words he had for them, as he walked up the hallway, away from them, towards the communal shower area.

Upon seeing Doug, John knew what had happened, but he was still slightly shocked at the scene before him as they entered the gym. Peter was on his side on the ground - still taped to the chair - surrounded by a pool of blood. Doug had had quite a workout. The tape had long since come off Peter's face and blood dribbled from his open mouth.

Closer inspection revealed that he had very few teeth left, most of them littered through the blood that surrounded him. His face was barely recognisable.

John had heard the phrase 'beaten to a pulp' many times before, but this was the first time he really felt it was fully applicable. He felt nauseous and found it hard to look at the sight of this ruined corpse, let alone 'clean up the mess'.

Sanjay wasted little time in getting things under way, producing a mop and bucket and a few sponges from the walk-in cupboard and bringing them over to Stuart and John. He placed the sponges into Stuart's hands and dropped the mop and bucket in front of John.

"Start cleaning up the blood. I'll be back in a minute, okay," he said casually, wandering out of the gym again.

Okay? John felt it was anything but okay. Cleaning up this bloody mess with a mop and sponges was very far from okay. But at the same time, what else could he do? What other option did they have?

This was the life he had chosen and he again rationalised the need to do what they had done - to set an example and prevent further confrontations and territorial disputes. This didn't make it any easier to stomach though. The bloody scene was right there in front of him and it was hard to deal with.

But deal with it he did. He switched into autopilot, swabbing the mop through the blood and draining it into the bucket, while Stuart repeatedly soaked and drained his sponges, the pair slowly filling the metal bucket.

They had gone some way towards cleaning up the blood, when Sanjay returned, carrying a roll of blue plastic sheeting under his arm. He proceeded to unroll it and lay it out on a blood-free area of the floor, near the door. He then marched over to the body, producing a butterfly knife, which he skilfully flicked open and began cutting the tape that was holding Peter to the chair.

John and Stuart continued cleaning up the blood, until Sanjay - having freed the body from the chair - requested their assistance.

"Right then, give us a hand."

The pair laid down their cleaning utensils and took hold of the same parts of Peter that they had held on the way down, picking him up and carrying him across the gym.

They dropped him in the middle of the plastic and Sanjay kneeled down and began rolling him in it. This did not take him long and he was soon ready to be moved again.

Although the body was heavy, it was a lot easier to carry than the squirming man they had brought in. John was still just going through the motions - doing what he had to do - without taking time to dwell on what had occurred. He just wanted the whole thing to be over.

They dropped the body into the car boot and after Sanjay made a quick trip back inside to get shovels, they got on the road, Sanjay driving through the darkness like he knew where he was going. John had little doubt that Sanjay had previous experience of situations like this and clearly had a deserted spot in mind - although there was no shortage of deserted places in the English countryside.

After driving for about five minutes, they turned up a narrow country lane and stopped beside a metal gate. Sanjay reached around, picking up the shovels from the back seat, produced a torch from the glove compartment and got out of the car.

As he made his way through the old gate, towards a large tree in the field - guided by torch light - he provided the perfect opportunity for John and Stuart to talk in private about what was going on. Instead, however, they sat in silence until Sanjay returned, staring through the windows into the black countryside.

He wasn't gone for long and as he returned and made his way round to the boot of the car, the pair stepped out and followed him. For the last time, they removed Peter from the boot and quickly marched him across the firm dry ground, to the tree where Sanjay had left the shovels.

Digging the grave was hard work, especially as they were all physically tired from carrying Peter around all night. When it was around a foot and a half deep, they stopped digging and rolled the plastic wrapped corpse into it.

Even with the light of the torch beside them, it was still hard to see what they were doing - no bad thing, as far as John was concerned. The less he could see, the less real it seemed.

It didn't take long to cover him over and they quickly made their way back to the car. A little bit more cleaning to do when they got back and their work would be done. Within a couple of hours they had plucked someone from their life - from the world - and made them disappear. No body, no witnesses and no risk of being caught, or of any reprisals.

Chapter Twenty-One

After five months, everything had become very routine for John. He was training hard and was - by his own declaration - in the best shape of his life. He was feeling lethal and his stamina had improved greatly since he first arrived in Manchester and began training in the gym in Nathan House.

Working at the weekends had become like second nature to him and even when violence was called for, it didn't really seem like a big deal. Violent action had become even more of a reflex for him than it had ever been.

He still occasionally thought about Peter. Thus far, that was the worst he'd seen, but by now he'd fully come round to the idea that extreme viciousness was sometimes a necessary evil of the drug world. Peter had died badly, but he had been given two physical warnings prior to that night and failed to heed them.

The lifestyle he was living had, to some extent, become more valuable to him than any moralistic problems he had with the actions sometimes required of him.

He was good friends with most of the guys now, his bank balance was very much healthier than it had ever been before and the majority of his time was spent doing exactly what he wanted. For him, it was like a dream.

He had never thought he would enjoy his life this much. Far removed from his door-to-door sales period, to say the least.

A break in the routine though, had come in the form of a message from Doug - delivered by Sanjay - that he was required for a special assignment that night. It was the first time he'd been called upon to work on a Tuesday night and he had no idea what he would have to do.

He knew other people had been called upon to do special jobs at various times, but they were never allowed to speak about them.

Everyone adhered very strictly to the rules of confidentiality, so John really did have no clue what he was needed for. All he did know was that Michael was also going to be involved in the assignment.

Since arriving in Manchester, he and Michael hadn't spent as much time together as he'd imagined they would. Not that they weren't friends anymore, far from it. He just spent a lot more time with various other guys than he did with Michael.

It was probably just because they'd lived in each other's pockets for so long in Australia, they didn't feel the need to do things together all the time.

On this occasion though, they were whiling the hours away together, until they were needed in Doug's office. It was now five o'clock and Doug didn't need them until eight. After a couple of hours of hogging the PlayStation 2 - playing Pro Evolution Soccer - things had predictably progressed to the pool table.

Michael's enthusiasm for the game was unrelenting. Like him, Michael was more than a little curious about what this assignment would involve.

"The waiting's a bastard isn't it?" said Michael.

He left the plastic triangle around the balls, obviously wanting to talk.

"It's gonna be a long three hours. I wish I knew what it was we have to do."

"I know, I'm very curious myself. It's bound to be a decent payday anyway."

"You think?" queried John.

Up to this point, he had not really considered the financial side of the situation.

"No doubt. This assignment is bound to have a price tag on it and we're certain to get a cut."

The bright side was suddenly getting brighter for John, who was naturally enticed by a big payday. Not that he wouldn't have been happy to do what was required of him anyway, but the potential financial gain made him more enthusiastic.

Michael now leaned back against the pool table with his cue standing up, balanced against his leg, before he continued.

"I hope we get a load of cash, coz I could really do with it."

This completely surprised John, as he had long since forgotten what financial worries were. He was contemplating looking into investing his money and was far away from being in dire need of cash.

"What do you mean? You should be loaded after being back five months."

"Well…"

Michael paused for a few seconds.

"Well, I haven't been too clever with my cash lately," Michael hesitantly confessed.

He paused again, clearly not enjoying this conversation, but forcing himself to continue.

"In fact mate, I'm a bit skint."

"Skint! What have you done with it all? How skint are you?"

Michael was looking at the ground, not wanting to make eye contact.

"I've made a few bad bets and now I'm down to minus fifteen grand."

"Oh fuck me! Fifteen grand! How long have you got?"

"Till Monday. I may need to borrow some money, if that's okay? I'll pay you back."

"Michael, you really will have to sort it out. I don't mind lending you money if you're in trouble, but you've got to get a grip. To be minus fifteen grand with the kind of money we make; you have a serious problem."

"Thanks John. This will be the last time it will happen. I've just got into a bit of a rut, but no more after this; seriously."

Michael turned back to the pool table, his spirits lifted and took the triangle from around the balls. He had clearly got what he'd wanted from the discussion.

This was not the first time John had encountered Michael's fondness for gambling. In Australia, there were times when the pair of them were on a very tight, almost non-existent budget and he would lose money making stupid bets, much to John's frustration.

He had no idea that it had developed into such a problem since their return. John could barely conceive of how someone could blow the kind of money they had coming to them every week and manage to be down to zero pounds, with a fifteen thousand pound debt.

After all they'd been through together, he had no problem with bailing Michael out. If it hadn't been for Michael, he wouldn't even have the money to lend him.

He was concerned though, that this might just be the beginning. Of course, he had to give him the benefit of the doubt and hope that he'd learned his lesson, but somehow he didn't think so.

Michael was bending down, lining up his cue to break, when John reached his hand on to the table and leaned down on the cue, getting his attention.

"This is the one and only time, okay Michael?"

"Honestly John, this is definitely it. I can't let it get like this again, so no more gambling. Really mate," Michael replied, with what appeared to be genuine sincerity.

John leaned off his cue and let him break. What more could he ask for than that?

Michael had said it and - knowing him as he did - John knew he meant it. Despite this, he still had a niggling feeling that this would not be the end of it.

Chapter Twenty-Two

Over the next three hours, there was no further mention of the gambling debts. The pair of them moved from the pool table, back to the PlayStation 2 and then back to the pool table again before eight o'clock.

When they arrived in Doug's office, they found Doug, Sanjay and Simon sitting around the desk talking.

"Right you two, take a seat and I'll tell you what we have to do," said Doug.

He stood up and leaned his hands on his desk, like a general ready to address his troops. If The Brotherhood was an army, then Doug was most certainly the general.

John and Michael quickly sat down and he began.

"Okay, first things first. You three are here because I believe that you are the three best men for this particular job. That's not to say you're my three favourite people, or my three best guys, you're just the three guys best suited to this job. I'm confident you can handle it.

That's how these special jobs go, so that's why different people get picked every time. Now, if all goes to plan, it shouldn't be too dangerous and there should be a nice healthy payout of about ten grand for each of you."

This information brought a smile to the faces of Simon, John and Michael; particularly Michael, who would now - if all went to plan - only have to borrow five thousand from John, which he knew would be no great imposition.

Sanjay didn't react and remained emotionless, obviously already well aware of the details of what they were about to do. If Doug was the general in the private army of The Brotherhood, then Sanjay was his lieutenant. Doug had clearly briefed him privately ahead of this meeting, possibly even consulting him when formulating the plan.

Doug continued his explanation of the mission at hand.

"The job is simple. Today, a few boys down in Moss Side made themselves a big score.

They sold a large quantity of ecstasy pills, which they managed to get into the country, and made themselves a very tidy profit. All we have to do is help them invest their money wisely - by giving it to us.

The deal only took place about half an hour ago and we know they are all still in the house together, probably celebrating their payday. We're going to secure the house, tie them up, find out where the money is, take it and get out of there, leaving no evidence."

No evidence clearly meant no living people, so it was obvious they would be killing these guys. This was not the primary concern in John's mind though; he was more concerned about the fact that they were going to be going into Moss Side to do a job like this.

Moss Side was an exceptionally rough, dangerous area and the kind of place where a white face stands out in the crowd. If anything were to go wrong, they could find themselves in a very bad situation, in the wrong place.

But ten thousand was a lot of money for a night's work. As he still occasionally did, John worked that out to be about twenty-seven thousand Australian dollars.

That was more money than he could have dared dream about having, during his year of travelling. There had been days when he'd been down to a dollar a day in spending money - aside from accommodation costs - which would mean a pint of milk, to stop him wasting away, and that was it.

Still, Moss Side. John was certainly not at his ease about the whole thing.

"I know the three of you - well, the four of you, including Sanjay - will be pleased to hear we'll be using guns tonight. You can each choose your favoured handgun, just as long as we have a silencer for it.

Silencers must remain on the guns at all times. We can't let anyone outside of the house know what's going on, or we could find ourselves in trouble.

Also, I'll give you each a pair of black leather gloves. These are to be worn at all times, once we get out of the car. I don't want any fingerprints left behind.

Simon, I assume you're still as handy as ever at picking locks?"

Simon nodded, with a cocky smirk on his face, obviously proud of his reputation for breaking and entering.

"Good. You and I will be going through the front door. The other three will be going in the back way. We're going to round them all up, get them in the kitchen at the back of the house and tape them up.

I'll go straight up the stairs, as soon as I get in, and sweep the rooms for strays. The rest of you, just rush through the ground floor and - as quickly and quietly as possible - get them in the kitchen.

If anyone gets noisy, lippy or doesn't move at the double; pistol-whip them, until they're not a problem. Any questions?"

Chapter Twenty-Three

It was just before ten o'clock, as they drove through a dark and quiet Moss Side, rain bouncing on the deserted concrete, in the glimmer of orange streetlights. They turned into a cul-de-sac and parked the car.

Doug, who was in the front passenger seat, turned around to give his chosen members of The Brotherhood a final briefing.

"Okay, it's the end house on the right. The lights are on in the living room, so it's likely most of them are in there. Remember, gloves and silencers on. John and Michael, you follow Sanjay and don't go until he gives the go ahead. Simon, we're going straight up to the front door, so pick the lock as quickly as you can, but don't go in until my signal."

He then turned back around and he and Sanjay synchronised their watches, with little difficulty.

"We go at one minute past exactly," he said, getting a nod from Sanjay.

Sanjay then - crowbar in hand - gestured for everyone to get out of the car.

They calmly walked the ten yards to the metal fence at the front of the house - trying not to appear conspicuous - before jumping over it, on to the small patch of grass, to the right of a concrete pathway leading up to the door. The blinds were closed, so as long as they didn't make a noise, they were unlikely to be seen. Doug and Simon went straight to the front door, while John and Michael followed Sanjay around the back.

The lights were out in the kitchen, but Sanjay gestured for them to kneel down below the kitchen window, while he knelt only inches away from the back door. He then stared at his watch, for what seemed to John to be a couple of minutes - but which was actually closer to thirty seconds - before stepping out, holding the crowbar with both hands.

Wedging it between the lock and the doorframe, he quickly opened the door, slamming his body weight through it. John and Michael swiftly followed, pistols in hand, as he made his way through the door joining the kitchen to the living room.

Simon was already in there, pointing his gun at the three middle-aged looking black men, who had jumped to their feet - from their seated positions facing the television - as they entered. John and Michael quickly moved into positions around the edge of the room, holding their guns in front of them with both hands, taking aim, surrounding the panicking men.

One of them managed to shout the words,

"What the fuck do - " before being cracked in the head with the crowbar by Sanjay.

He dropped to the ground, the side of his head bleeding and the other two held up their hands, cowering away from him, saying nothing. Doug then emerged; gun by his side, giving the thumbs up that upstairs was all clear.

It didn't take long to get the three men taped up in the kitchen. They struggled very little, obviously fearful of a blow from the crowbar - or indeed, being shot. There was no doubt that the silencers conveyed their readiness to use the guns. After all, if they'd just brought guns to scare and threaten, why bother attaching them?

John was surprised at how little resistance the three men had shown, considering the money at stake and the fact that these were three big guys from Moss Side, who looked like they weren't used to taking this kind of abuse. The kind of guys who - if you were keen on not getting mugged - you might cross the street to avoid. Yet there they were, taped up, face down on the kitchen floor, about to get robbed and killed.

So far it seemed too easy, but they still had to find out where the money was. Simon and Michael had conducted a fruitless search of the house, so it seemed they would have to be told where it was.

"That one," said Doug, pointing to the biggest of the three guys.

This was also the one who had been hit in the head and the one who seemed most likely to be the gang leader. He had obviously been selected for special attention.

"Pick him up and sit him on the kitchen bench."

All four of them picked him up and put him in position, while Doug peeked through the closed kitchen blinds, into the back garden.

Despite the fact that it seemed unlikely anyone would have seen what was happening, he seemed slightly uneasy and was certainly eager to get the whole thing over with and get out of Moss Side.

The guy was sitting upright on the bench, leaning back against the kitchen table; wrists and ankles tightly bound, a strip of elephant tape covering his mouth. The blood was still dripping from the wound on the side of his head, although it didn't look too serious - not that it mattered.

Doug walked over to him, leaned downwards - so that he was at eye level with him - and put his finger on his mouth, to indicate that he was not to make a sound. He then pulled off the piece of elephant tape from his mouth, in one swift movement.

"When I ask you to speak, speak quietly. Any shouting or screaming and you'll be shot. Any attempt to break free, you'll be shot. Understand?" Doug said abruptly, with a no nonsense tone in his voice.

In keeping with the minimum noise, minimum talking theme of the instructions, the guy nodded in response.

"Good, alright then, let's get down to it. You know why we're here and you know what I want. You came into some money today and I've come for it. Now, no offence, but I don't like Moss Side much; it's not my cup of tea, so I'd like to leave this place. Of course, I can't leave without my money, so if you'd like to hurry things along a bit and tell me where it is, I can be on my way."

Doug stood upright and turned away from the guy, taking a few steps and then turning back to him.

"Well?" he asked sternly.

The guy just sat there, staring blankly in front of him, not saying a word and with a look of defiant determination on his face, giving the impression he did not plan on saying a word, no matter what. Understandable, John thought, considering he'd only had the money in his possession for a couple of hours and they were waving guns and trying to take it from him.

Doug was not in the mood to waste time though and immediately gave a nod to Sanjay, who walked out through the back door.

"You're gonna tell me, you know. You may have a pretty bad time for the next few minutes, but you will tell me. You're going to tell me everything," Doug told him, menacingly.

He then just stood, staring at the guy for a few seconds, before stepping forward to him and punching him full in the nose, breaking it and sending blood streaming down his face. Then, like before, he turned, took a few steps away from him and turned to face him again.

He was still coming to terms with the blow to the nose, gasping for air through his bloody mouth, water pouring from his eyes.

"What's your name?" was Doug's next question, asked like a schoolteacher demanding an answer from a pupil.

The answer once again was not forthcoming and Doug stepped forward, punching him again, this time in his right eye. A trickle of blood ran down from his eyebrow, slowly rolling down his cheek.

Again, Doug took a few steps away from him, and then turned to face him.

Without taking his eyes off the bloodied target of his questioning, he spoke to one of his own gang members.

"Simon, find out his name."

Within a few seconds of searching his trouser pockets, Simon produced a wallet and threw it to Doug. He opened it and had a quick look through it, before announcing the name of the prisoner.

"Gordon. Your name is Gordon. Don't you feel better now that I know a little bit more about you Gordon? How about telling me where my fucking money is Gordon?"

It occurred to John that Gordon might have been known by some sort of street name to other criminals and to his narcotics customers. Gordon didn't sound to John like an appropriate name for a gangster/drug dealer from Moss Side.

At this point, John felt sure that Gordon was going to tell Doug where the money was, and sooner rather than later. Doug was a very determined man and he liked to win, even if this time the game was interrogation.

NEIL WALKER

Chapter Twenty-Four

Sanjay re-entered the kitchen, making Gordon's fate look even bleaker.

In his left hand, he was carrying a black plastic bucket, with the sharp end of a circular saw peering out the top of it.

In his right hand, there was a pair of plastic safety goggles. These were obviously to be worn while using the circular saw.

As Gordon saw what he was carrying, the terror was visible on his face. He now knew that he would have to withstand a lot more than just a beating, if he wanted to keep his money.

Sanjay placed the bucket on the floor, directly in between Doug and Gordon and threw Doug the goggles. Then - as if what he had just brought into the room did not deserve a mention - he walked back out through the back door, without saying a word.

What was he off to get now, John thought, a flamethrower?

Then, for maybe ten seconds after Sanjay made his exit, Doug didn't say anything. He just stood with his arms folded and a smile on his face, looking at the bucket, then up at Gordon, then at the bucket, then up at Gordon.

This continued until it seemed likely that Gordon would break his self-imposed vow of silence just to say, 'What are you going to do to me?' He didn't though and Doug put him out of his misery - and into more misery.

"A circular saw Gordon. It can be used to cut through a variety of things; for example, muscle tissue or bone. Granted, that's not what most DIY enthusiasts use it for, but that's what we'll use it for tonight - coz tonight Gordon, this is your life. This is the pivotal moment in your life.

You see my friend, this could be your last day as an able-bodied person. You get to decide.

Do you ever want to stand up on two legs again? Do you ever want to write a letter, or have a wank, or ride a bike again? Is it really worth it Gordon? Is it really worth the money?"

All eyes were on Gordon - the taped up, bleeding, centre of attention. Waiting for him to give in, to tell all, to concede that whatever Doug was going to do to him with the circular saw, was more than he could bear.

To say that yes, he did want to stand on two legs again and his health was more important than the money.

In his mind, John was just willing him to talk. Despite the knowledge that Gordon and his two associates were dead no matter what, he did not relish the idea of being involved in, or witnessing, this macabre spectacle.

It seemed though, that despite being visibly shaken, Gordon was determined to continue his silent protest.

"Well, let's see shall we? Let's see if it's worth the money. I'm going to tell you what we're gonna do, then I'll give you another opportunity to tell me where the money is. If you choose not to take this opportunity, then the tape goes back over your mouth and we go to work. Fair enough?"

Predictably, there was no response from Gordon and Doug swiftly continued with the process.

"We'll start with your left foot, cutting somewhere around the middle of your shin, still leaving you a decent stump. Your foot goes in the bucket. Then, if you still don't want to talk to us, we'll take your right foot, then your left hand, and then your right hand.

Now, if by this time what's left of you still does not feel talkative, we'll cut off your fucking head - just to spite you - and throw it in the bucket, with your hands and feet. Then we'll go to work on one of your little girlfriends here."

Sanjay was back, this time carrying a pile of medical gowns and rubber gloves, which he immediately began distributing, one gown and one pair of gloves to each of them.

"You'll have a minute or two while we get ready, to think it over," were the last words from Doug to Gordon.

They all began putting on the medical gowns over their clothes as quickly as they could.

John was reminded of watching ER. He wasn't a huge fan, but no matter which hostel he and Michael had stayed in while they were in Australia, ER had always been a firm favourite in the TV room.

Despite the fact that they were supposed to have been off having adventures and seeing Australia, they had spent many a night - and many a day - lounging in front of the television. He had never imagined he would be in a situation where he'd need to wear one of the surgical gowns from the operating theatres in ER.

Mind you, there was a lot about this situation he might never have believed he would be a part of. It was happening all the same.

Chapter Twenty-Five

"Flip the other two over, so they can watch," instructed Doug, as he plugged in the saw.

The other four rolled the two guys - who had been facing the floor - over, sitting them slightly upright against the wall, giving them a perfect view of what was to happen to Gordon.

"Sanjay, go and stick some music on; pretty loud, but not so loud that the neighbours come knocking," was Doug's next instruction.

Sanjay made his way into the living room, in search of a stereo.

"Anything you'd like to tell me Gordon, before I start this up?" asked Doug, wielding the circular saw, ready to start cutting.

Still nothing.

John was very surprised. This guy was actually going to make them cut him up.

And so it began.

"Right you three, tape his mouth thoroughly; I mean wrap the tape around his head three or four times. We don't want him screaming the house down. Then lie him down in the middle of the floor."

They quickly did as Doug directed, Michael taping his mouth, wrapping it round his head as instructed and then the three of them manoeuvred him on to the floor.

He didn't struggle too much. He seemed almost resigned to the inevitable.

Dance floor drum n' bass was Sanjay's choice from the CDs available. It came blaring through from the living room, marking Sanjay's return to the kitchen.

He obviously knew the drill, walking straight over to Gordon and sitting on his stomach, pushing his hands down on his shoulders and giving orders to his three fellow Brotherhood members.

"Two of you take his legs, separate them and lean all your fucking weight on them. His legs don't move!"

The three of them looked at each other, wondering who the two would be. Doug quickly chipped in, making it clear that it was not up to them; it was up to him.

He was the man in charge.

"Michael, keep your gun on the two lovebirds."

By default, this left Simon and John as the ones to help pin Gordon down.

John wasn't sure why Michael got to cover the other two. Maybe he'd paid his dues in the past, or maybe it was just because he wasn't as physically strong. Whatever the reason, Michael had certainly got the golden ticket.

John and Simon got down on the ground and took a firm grip of Gordon's legs, Simon producing his infamous Stanley knife and cutting through the elephant tape binding his ankles.

Once his legs were separated, he started to struggle more and all three men had to work hard to keep him still. For him though, there was no escape.

Doug spoke to him one last time, giving him one more opportunity, as he stood over him with the saw.

"Last chance Gordon."

Gordon gave no response, looking straight up at the ceiling.

"Sanjay, if he looks like he wants to say something, signal me to stop."

And that was all there was to say. Doug pulled the goggles over his eyes and switched on the circular saw.

He started with the left leg, which Simon was holding. Simon gripped it at the knee, leaning all his body weight on the top of the leg, leaving Doug with a clear target.

John was half expecting a last minute reprieve, a change of heart from Gordon or just something to stop this going ahead. It was not forthcoming.

It amazed John how easily the circular saw cut through his leg, although he couldn't really see very much, as he had to squint his eyes and duck his head down, because of all the spraying blood. There was a lot of blood and it was spraying in all directions, like a haze of warm red raindrops.

He found it slightly surreal to be a part of something so grotesque.

It was almost like he couldn't connect with the fact that it was actually happening. That the liquid spattering his face was actually someone's blood. That the saw was really cutting through someone's leg.

He now felt sure that one leg would be enough, that that was as far as they'd have to go.

As Doug held out the bucket with Gordon's foot in it for him to look at, however, he just firmly closed his eyes and looked away. He was in complete agony and could actually see his own foot look back at him from the bottom of a bucket, but still he had nothing to say.

With each successive limb, John kept thinking this has to be it, he couldn't take any more, but still he maintained his stubborn silence, until it was clear that they would not be hearing from Gordon.

John had thought a lot of blood had come from the arms and legs, but as Doug sawed into his neck, then he really saw what a lot of blood was. It went everywhere, covering the already blood-soaked foursome.

Michael had managed to avoid getting too badly covered, by taking up a position as far away from Gordon as possible, while still being able to keep his gun on the other two.

Doug placed the head face up in the bucket, on top of the feet and hands, and walked over to the two remaining prisoners. They already looked totally terrorised, spattered with blood, tears streaming down their faces, both seeming to have lost bladder control.

Seeing their friend's decapitated head in a bucket with an assortment of his limbs, however, seemed to take them to a new level of complete terror.

Doug set the bucket down on the ground and held his forefinger up to his mouth, signalling for quiet when he removed the tape from their mouths. He then reached forward and pulled the piece of tape from the mouth of the one nearest him.

The second the tape was off his mouth, without any prompting, the guy rushed out the information they wanted, in a quiet and shivering voice.

"Big bedroom, in-built cupboard, under the floorboards."

He spoke with a sense of urgency that made it clear he really didn't want to suffer the same fate as his friend.

Sanjay immediately headed out of the kitchen, through the living room and up the stairs. For the next minute, no one in the kitchen moved or said a word, Doug just staring at the cowering pair of broken men in front of him.

Then, Sanjay came bounding back down the stairs and made his way through to the kitchen, with a black sports bag in his hand and a smile on his face. He had already inspected the contents, which he revealed to Doug, holding the unzipped bag open.

The other three couldn't fail to notice the large quantity of bundles of fifty pound notes contained within. John guessed it would have been at least one hundred and fifty thousand pounds, probably a lot more. He couldn't be specific with the brief glimpse he got, but it was a lot of money.

Sanjay zipped up the bag, set it down on the ground and took off his blood drenched medical gown, prompting everyone else to do the same. It was time to go, apart from Doug's final instructions.

"Michael, look after these two. Sanjay, turn off the music."

Without hesitation, Michael fired a shot from his silenced pistol into the head of each of the remaining pair of rival gang members, shooting the one without tape on his mouth first.

Sanjay hit the stop button on the CD player in the living room and the five of them left through the back door. Their work here was done.

They got paid that night, ten thousand as promised, in fifty pound notes. It was a big pay out, although John couldn't help but feel a little resentment, considering how much money had been in the bag. Of course, he didn't complain.

Michael seemed more than happy with the money; especially after he got his hands on half of John's, taking care of his gambling debts.

NEIL WALKER

Chapter Twenty-Six

John had gone home to Belfast for Christmas to see his family, under instructions to be back by New Year's Eve. Even if he could have stayed at home for New Year's, he would still have gone back to England.

According to the others, it was the biggest payday of the year, which obviously made sense. His experience had led him to believe that people always went overboard on New Year's.

If they would usually take one or two pills each weekend, on New Year's they would take maybe four or five pills and a gram of coke. Basically, everyone would push the boat out.

There was no way John would have let himself miss out on that kind of money. Besides, he had also been told that the after parties on New Year's were the stuff of legend.

After a somewhat pathetic New Year's Eve in a Perth pub the previous year, he was keen to be a part of a legendary New Year's Eve party.

He had spent five days in Belfast, not really doing much of anything. Christmas was quiet, just himself, his mother and his grandfather. Despite his limited cooking skills, he had helped his mother with the dinner.

A couple of solo trips to the cinema and a bit of shopping and that was about all he got up to.

The phone had been tormenting him the entire time he was back, serving as a constant reminder that he should phone his friends and arrange to see them. He'd been away from home for nearly a year and a half and would have received a hero's welcome, getting inundated with free drinks and free pills.

Despite this, in five days he didn't call or meet a single one of them.

He wasn't really sure why either; he just couldn't bring himself to do it. Maybe he couldn't face making up lies the whole time, about what he was up to in Manchester. He'd certainly grown weary of lying to his mother.

Or maybe he just couldn't face the idea of sitting down with his friends and pretending to be the person he was the last time they saw him. He couldn't picture many of them living the life that he'd been living since he'd been in England; doing what he'd done.

Whatever the reason, he had arrived back from Belfast without contacting any of his old friends or going to any of his old haunts. He just put it down to having moved on and didn't really dwell on it too much.

His mother had been very emotional upon his departure. She did not go with him to the airport, as she didn't think she could handle it.

She didn't want to make a sobbing spectacle of herself. Nevertheless, she had broken down in the house before he left.

Understandable really, her only child having not been home in so long and then just stopping by for a flying visit. He knew it was hard for her, particularly with her not having re-married; she must have been very lonely.

But being in Belfast full-time and trying to go back to wasting his time in a dead-end job was more than he could bear.

Besides, although it was never really talked about, he knew that he could never just walk away from The Brotherhood. The longest anyone had really been away for after joining - that he knew of anyway - was Michael. And that was only because Doug very much trusted him and it was obvious that he'd be back and keep his mouth shut.

Even then, trust or no trust, if Michael had wanted to leave for good, John believed he'd be six feet under - or at least two feet under.

John had long since accepted this harsh reality and was fine with it, as he wouldn't have left even if he could. An ordinary life was too hard, too daunting.

He did, however, vow to do his best to make more trips home. Just fly home for a few days during the week, every now and again, when there was nothing going on. It wasn't like money was a problem and he often had the time.

For now though, he put Belfast out of his mind.

Walking back into Doug's place felt more like a homecoming for him than arriving back in Northern Ireland. He felt a sense of relief as he dropped his bags down in his room and collapsed back on to the bed.

For a couple of minutes he just lay there, content to stare up at the ceiling, before he was disturbed by a knock at the door.

He waited a couple of seconds, sighed and responded unenthusiastically.

"Yeah."

Despite the uninterested tone of the reply, it still prompted Stuart to come into the room.

"Well, good Christmas?" was his first line of conversation, one that John knew he would be hearing a lot through the day.

"Not bad. And yourself?" was John's perfunctory and non-specific response.

Stuart had expected to be inundated with drunken tales of Belfast but decided, as John was not forthcoming, to wait until he wanted to talk about it and instead tell him about events in the house while he was away.

"Good yeah. On Christmas Day, there were only Dave, James and myself in the house. Doug was around, but mostly in his own part of the house. It was alright, but on Boxing Day the place was rocking.

People started drinking and taking drugs really early; we're talking cocaine on the cornflakes here, washed down with a can of Stella. Then, in the afternoon, we were all in the screening room for The Italian Job, followed by Escape To Victory. It was a totally drunken Christmassy experience."

Doug had a section of the house that was pretty much his own. Rooms that he kept for himself and had locked most of the time. No one ever questioned this, as it was only fair; it was his house.

One of these rooms was the screening room, a scaled down cinema, which he had installed; complete with a small cinema screen, projector, a reasonable collection of film reels and about fifty authentic cinema seats. Apparently he'd bought them from a cinema that was about to be demolished.

Very rarely did Doug invite everybody in for group screenings - mostly just on special occasions.

"Everyone managed to make it out dealing that night," Stuart continued, "although a few people were in a very dubious state. There was a lot of speed taken to get people out the door. Needless to say, most of the guys were back pretty early, but the party afterwards was something else.

You missed out, but don't worry tonight will be better. Everyone is well up for it tonight."

Stuart was obviously very excited about New Year's Eve, much in contrast to John. Although he was glad to be back, he didn't really feel up to the excess and partying that lay ahead. Rather than finding Stuart's excitement annoying, however, he sensed that it could become infectious - and he wanted to be made excited about New Year's.

"You certainly seem well up for it," he commented, prompting Stuart to enthuse further.

"Oh, I am totally up for it. My head was a bit delicate for a few days after Boxing Night, but now I'm back together and ready to wreck my head again. Working will be a laugh tonight as well, coz it looks like we'll be working together."

"How do you know that?"

"Well, you and I have to go up and see Doug in the office in about five minutes and that's what he seems to be doing; telling people where they're going tonight and who with. I'm assuming, coz we're seeing him together, we're working together."

It did seem likely and after five minutes of listening to Stuart talk about how 'up for it' he was, they made their way to Doug's office to find out for sure.

"Okay boys, take a seat," said Doug.

He was sounding almost as chirpy as Stuart.

"John, good to see you made it back from Beirut in one piece," he quipped.

Comments like this had no impact whatsoever on John, who had heard a lifetime's worth of these witticisms on his travels. Plus he could tell it was meant in good humour, as was Doug's way.

"I'm giving you boys a late Christmas present, you'll be pleased to hear. You should both have an extremely lucrative night tonight - in Manhattan Nights."

Straight away the pair of them were grinning from ear to ear.

"I thought it was only fair, after you missed out on working the place the last time; so take advantage and work hard. You really should make a killing tonight. It opens at eight thirty, so you'll need to be down there - in the queue - for about half seven. The club is running right through till seven in the morning so don't hurry back. There's no hurry for the party, coz I'm pretty sure it will run on well into New Year's Day.

Also, I've told everyone to come down to the screening room for about four. I'm going to stick on Human Traffic, to get everyone up for it and in party mood. It's our biggest night of the year and I want everyone psyched up for a good one."

John was a big fan of Human Traffic. It had come out in the cinema at around the same time as his ecstasy love affair had really got into full swing and he'd been to see it seven or eight times. One weekend, he'd gone to see it on a Saturday evening, before going clubbing and then again on the Sunday afternoon, to help him through his comedown.

If anything could get him in the right frame of mind, it was watching that. Just the knowledge that he'd be watching it that day had lifted his spirits, especially coupled with the fact that he and Stuart had been given Manhattan Nights.

"Right then, I'll just get you guys sorted out with a big pile of drugs and you'll be all set. Okay?"

Chapter Twenty-Seven

They had certainly arrived in Manhattan Nights with a lot of drugs. It quickly became clear, however, that they would probably sell them all quite easily.

It was only half past eleven and already John was running low on cocaine. The fact that he was definitely going to save some for himself meant he had even less. It was New Year's Eve and he would not do without cocaine - and the rest.

His mood had perked up dramatically by this point. This was due to a combination of an enjoyable and highly motivational viewing of Human Traffic that afternoon, complete with beers and the fact that the club had a very lively atmosphere and no shortage of attractive women to look at. The effects of the Christmas tree embossed ecstasy pill he had consumed in the queue while waiting to get in had also been a factor.

If John's mood had picked up, Stuart's had pretty much stayed on a level since that morning, his enthusiasm never wavering. Unlike John, he had decided to hold off on the drugs, until later that night.

John knew Stuart was doing the sensible thing and would have preferred to do likewise, but he hated the tedium of queuing and Human Traffic had really whetted his appetite for some pills. In fact, as he stood at the edge of the dance floor, he was contemplating taking his next one - or half of it at least.

He could see Stuart from where he was standing, conducting his business at the back of the stage area with a fair degree of subtlety, the type of subtlety that had eluded John throughout the night. He had been as blatant as a man under the influence of an ecstasy pill, but he didn't care. The last time they'd compared notes, he'd sold more than Stuart anyway, although his figures couldn't be trusted to be entirely accurate; once again, because of the ecstasy.

As he bit into his second Christmas tree pill - swallowing half and keeping half for later - he received a tap on the shoulder, turning around to see an attractive young blonde woman in a mini-dress. John couldn't help but blatantly look her up and down, as he washed down his half pill with a swig from his can of Red Bull.

She was only about five foot seven in heels and gestured for John to lean down a bit, so she could speak into his ear. John obliged.

"I need two pills and a gram of charlie," she said, just loud enough to be heard over the music.

John cupped his free hand over her ear and responded in a loud voice directly into it.

"No problem, that's eighty quid."

Usually, this would be the point where they'd quickly organise their money/drugs and make a discrete exchange. Not so this time, the girl beckoning him to lean down again. This time she was a bit louder.

"I don't have any money."

If he hadn't heard it so clearly, he would have thought he had misunderstood.

"Sorry, I need eighty quid."

Each time he leaned down to hear her speak, he took full advantage of his opportunity to leer at her cleavage and legs, without fear of being caught.

"I only just had enough money to pay in tonight. I'm pretty skint after Christmas, but my mates are gonna be partying all night on pills and they don't have any spare."

Spare pills were not too common. People could always find a use for their pills.

"Listen, I'd like to help you, but there are too many people here with money to spend. They get the drugs."

This time she seemed to stop and think for a second, before responding.

"What about if you give me something I want and I give you something you want?"

John needed no explanation of what she meant and was very much in favour of what she had in mind. He only had one question for her.

"Where?"

She took him by the hand, leading him across the dance floor, towards the toilets. With no alcohol or ecstasy in his system, he might not have felt entirely comfortable marching into the crowded gents toilets with a girl on his arm, but as it was, it didn't faze him in the slightest. Receiving a few dirty looks and one comment of "Go on my son," along the way, they marched straight into a vacant cubicle and locked the door behind them.

The majority of the guys in the toilets were lingering, having drug-fuelled conversations - rather than actually using the facilities - so finding a vacant cubicle was quite easy.

After locking the door, the young woman went straight to work, not saying a word or even looking him the eye, as she turned to face him and got down on her knees. She masturbated him until his penis was hard - which didn't take long - and then put it in her mouth. At first, she went slowly and John couldn't believe how good it felt.

It had been a couple of months since he'd had any kind of sexual encounter with a woman and he'd always been a great believer in the view that oral sex is more enjoyable than sexual intercourse.

One night in Australia, himself, Michael and a couple of Canadian guys had debated the topic for almost two hours; fuelled by beer and Bourbon. They had been entirely divided, he and one of the Canadians preferring fellatio, with the other two arguing that intercourse was better. Inevitably the debate concluded with an 'each to their own' agreement, but John was in little doubt of his feelings on the matter.

He wasn't sure whether this attractive young woman was particularly good at performing the act, or whether he was just enjoying it so much because it had been so long and he was on pills. Either way, he was having fun.

He certainly had no qualms about paying for it, having sampled at least his fair share of prostitutes in Thailand on his way to Australia, although technically he wasn't actually paying this woman money. Eighty pounds worth of drugs was quite a lot for a blowjob though. In Thailand, eighty pounds could hire two women to be of service sexually and around the house for a month and still leave change for groceries.

Despite feeling it was slightly expensive, John wasn't complaining, as she went faster and faster and he gripped her head with his right hand, leaning his left against the wall of the cubicle for support. He thought about warning her as he was about to climax, just in case she didn't want to swallow. Such etiquette he decided did not apply in the situation where it was costing him. He wanted to come in her mouth and did - emphatically.

As it was, she didn't seem to mind, holding it in her mouth until he'd finished ejaculating. John was pleased about this, as any sperm stains on his trousers would have been a thorn in his side for the rest of the night. He would have been open to ridicule if anyone were to see them and they would have reduced his chances of pulling, which this encounter had definitely put him in the mood for.

After pulling up and fastening his trousers, he reached a gram of coke and two pills out of his jacket pocket and placed them in her hand. Out of a mix of politeness and curiosity, John felt compelled to ask her something.

"What's your name anyway?"

"What does it matter?" she replied, smiling as she opened the latch on the door and left the cubicle.

John had also been wondering about her age, as he was guessing she was around eighteen or nineteen, but couldn't be sure. And why not tell him her name?

As she had pointed out though, what did it matter? The exchange of goods for services had been made and they'd both gone away happy.

Maybe it was her way of empowering herself to snub his question, he thought, but he really didn't care. He just hoped she'd run out of drugs before the night was over and they could strike another deal.

As he stepped out of the cubicle, he received a round of applause - from those who'd been paying attention - as well as a couple of pats on the back and one enquiry as to whether or not he knew where to get any pills. He sold the guy what he needed in plain view of everyone, sparking something of a feeding frenzy from others on the look out for drugs.

John left the toilets with an extra four hundred pounds in his pocket and an experience of oral sex under his belt. As far as he was concerned, New Year's Eve could not have been going any better.

NEIL WALKER

Chapter Twenty-Eight

It was seven thirty a.m. before Stuart and John made it back to Nathan House, Stuart having driven home at a fairly high speed, while coming up on his second pill. Not the safest way to travel, but John was in no state to care.

They'd both had a ball at Manhattan Nights, although were both disappointed at not having been taken home by a young lady.

Stuart had been kissing an attractive woman at different points throughout the night, but hadn't been able to find her at the end - despite a lengthy and slightly desperate search. John hadn't managed to get a kiss all night, although he had managed to secure a second instalment of fellatio from the same sexy young woman as before, this time at a cost of only two pills. He felt he'd got better value the second time, although he never did find out her name.

John had already gone through three pills, a number of dabs of coke - probably amounting to half a gram - and a wrap of speed, snorted during the drive home. As they entered the main hall, he was still in the hedonistic frame of mind to take a lot more. Michael and Ben were sitting near the door and immediately jumped out of their seats and ran over to John and Stuart, hugging them and wishing them a happy New Year.

The party was well under way and from a glance around the hall it seemed everyone was there, or certainly most of them. Trev was at the front, behind the decks, in the middle of a hard house set and there were an unusual amount of people dancing.

It seemed - like the outside world - the world inside this house had succumbed to the irresistible temptation of a night of universal excess. For once, there was no one playing pool. All too fucked, thought John.

The four of them sat around the table that Ben and Michael had been snorting coke and speed from for the past hour. Despite their previous indulgence, the table was still very well stocked.

Two mirrors, side by side, each covered with lines of white powder; laid out running parallel, horizontally across each one, like a freshly ploughed field. Lying in between the two mirrors was a credit card, lightly dusted with white powder, and a cylindrical metal snorting device, which John was sure belonged to Ben.

Ben was very keen on his drug apparatus, also owning a wide variety of bongs and pipes.

"So, what's what?" asked John, admiring the bounty before him.

Michael pointed to the mirror on his left.

"Coke."

He then pointed to the mirror on his right.

"Speed."

He followed this information with two very dangerous words.

"Help yourselves."

All John had left on him were a few pills, about half a gram of coke and one more wrap of speed and he would have to save something from that stash to help him through - what would inevitably be - a horrific comedown. He immediately knelt down by the table and - using the metal device - snorted a line of cocaine.

As soon as he'd finished, Stuart followed suit, so John surmised that he must also have all but sold out. Either that, or he just felt like taking advantage of this drug-induced generosity.

It had been a very prosperous night in Manhattan Nights, where John could have actually sold more than he did - if he'd had more with him - so he had little doubt that Stuart's reserves were low.

As they both sat back up in their chairs, sniffing and letting the effects of the coke kick in, Dave emerged back into the hall and joined them, having just been away at the toilet.

"Alright you two, Happy New Year," he said, as he sat down.

John and Stuart responded with an almost simultaneous, "Happy New Year mate!"

Dave lasted in his seat for all of five seconds, before getting down on his knees for a quick line of speed. Like the other four, he too was very much under the influence. They were five big-pupilled, teeth-grinding, fidgety, over-enthusiastic messes.

Dave was from Peckham and was the only black guy to be part of The Brotherhood. Indeed, he was the only person of any race other than white - apart from Sanjay - to be a member.

He kept himself to himself more than most of them; not that he was unsociable or rude, he was just one of the people who could be found around Nathan House the least. When the time arrived to take stimulant drugs, however, he really came to life and would always make his presence felt.

He turned his speed-fuelled attentions to John, asking, "Tonight go well then mate? I bet you made a killing in Manhattan Nights; you must have sold a fucking load."

"Big time!" John replied, "I have never seen anything like it. I've sold about ten grand's worth of stuff, which puts five grand in my pocket for a night's work and I had a fucking ball. One of the best nights I've ever had out in a club."

"I had a good night too man. Sold way more than usual - although not as much as you - and managed to get a fuck outside."

By now, the other three were engrossed in a separate conversation, along similar lines. A five-way discussion would never work for long with them in this state. Too little opportunity to talk, and they were talking incessantly.

"I got two blowjobs throughout the night, in the bogs, off the same gorgeous young lady. Cost me four pills and a gram of coke, all told, but it was gooood."

"Yeah mate, I've done that before - got women to pay me in kind. It made me feel like such a dirty bastard…it was fantastic! And I'd do it again!"

As they both laughed, John decided to put a ridiculous question to Dave - one that he'd never been in a detached enough state to ask him before. With tongue firmly in cheek, he made his enquiry.

"So Dave, while we're talking about sex and stuff, I have to ask. I know it's probably a stupid question and I'm not being racist or anything like that, but is it true what they say about black guys? Y'know, their dicks?"

Dave sat forward in his chair, with a veneer of sincerity, and kept a straight face while delivering his answer.

"John, I'll tell it to you straight, even though it's personal. Having just taken a piss, I can honestly say that my dick is the size of a peanut, with all the fuckin' speed I've had tonight."

They both erupted with laughter, lying back in their seats.

John was then drawn towards the conversation the other three were having, when he overheard Ben mention having worked in a call centre.

"Which call centre did you work in?" he interrupted.

"It was the call centre for a bank; just doing transactions and stuff. Did it for almost a year," Ben replied.

John gave him a look of sympathy. He could very much empathise with his experience.

"I know about the call centre thing mate. I worked in one for a phone company and fucking hell - I was straight out of university and got a job as a carefully monitored fucking robot. Christ I hated that job!"

"Tell me about it John, those were dark days. But thank fuck we will never have to walk that path and take that shit again. No more anal retentive, trained monkey, bollocky fucking jobs. Coz instead, we live like kings and party all night!"

This rousing comment prompted a cheer from all five of them, followed by them all kneeling down around the table for another line.

As the hours went by, the drugs ran low, the conversation slowed down and each successive line was washed down with a glass of champagne - fitting for the occasion - something occurred to John.

"Where's Doug? Has anyone seen Doug?"

The other four shook their heads.

"That's weird, for him not to make an appearance. Did anyone go up to see him in the office?"

"Rory did," said Michael.

"He was telling me earlier. He was one of the first back, but the office was locked and no one answered when he knocked."

"I suppose he just wants to sort all that shit out tomorrow," Ben chipped in.

He then continued with his attempt to explain and excuse Doug's absence.

"I mean he knew people would be coming back way later than usual and way more fucked."

"Makes sense," Michael agreed, keen to back Ben and justify Doug's behaviour.

John was not satisfied.

"Regardless of the drugs, sorting out money and all that shit, you'd think he'd be around for the party and say Happy New Year and whatever."

A couple of unenthusiastic nods were the only response from the other four, who possibly sensed that John was about to pass negative judgement on Doug and wanted no part of it. John was not foolish enough to do any such thing.

If he ever did think badly of Doug, he would never vocalise it; that would be very dangerous. It would be like making derogatory remarks to someone about their best friend, no matter who in the organisation he said it to.

Doug had respect beyond respect from these guys and from John too. He didn't really feel anything negative towards him for not making an appearance; he was more just a little bit disappointed.

And it made him wonder if Doug was too busy or too tired to join the party, or if he was just trying to remain aloof, to some extent? After all, he rarely ever came down to the after-parties.

He didn't think about it too much, however, thinking too much being beyond him at this point. Instead, he focused on drinking like it was a mission, passing the stage of champagne and entering whiskey territory - all this alcohol being a prelude to a large dose of sleeping pills and tranquillisers.

They had to make the most of whatever sleep they could get, as when they woke up, they knew there would be hell to pay for their celebrations.

Chapter Twenty-Nine

With Valentine's Day looming during the week and no regular girlfriends to occupy Stuart and John, they were making plans to go out and reap the harvest of single, desperate women. They were in high spirits, as they'd both just got back to the house, having finished dealing for Saturday night, and could party without consequences, knowing their work was done.

Neither of them had been going too overboard on drugs and alcohol since New Year's Eve though. They had both suffered nightmarish comedowns, which had lingered for days, and had been put off over-indulgence - if only for a couple of months.

Not too many people were back at the house as yet, no one was DJing and the CD in the stereo wasn't playing too loud, so it was easy to talk, as they reclined in their La-Z-Boys facing each other.

"I reckon Planet Earth is the way to go," suggested Stuart.

He was referring to the eighties retro club, always filled wall to wall with students.

"Despite the fact that I hate the eighties, I'm inclined to agree man. The talent in there can be great sometimes and on Valentine's night, it will be a major meat market. The trick will be finding girls who want to take us back to their place, rather than us take them back to ours."

"Luck of the draw I'm afraid, unless you are prepared to ask them early in the night about it, but that could backfire and earn you a slap in the face."

"A slap in the face would be more contact than I've had with a woman since New Year's Eve."

"Do you ever think we should move out of here and get a flat, for the sake of our sex lives, coz we really are on bread and water half the time?"

John had given it a lot of thought, particularly during the comedown week following New Year's, when he just wanted space and to be away from the scene of the crime. It was getting to him a bit, that he lived in the same place as he partied and that he trained in and did most of his socialising in.

He was quick to point out to Stuart the logical reasons for staying where they were, however, having already decided against moving out in his own mind.

"We could move out, but we'd be moving out of a rent-free, bill-free mansion and into a pay-for little flat. Even though this place has it's down side, it's too hard to leave."

"That's true mate. It's been proven, any of the lads who ever move in for a while rarely move out. Like you say, it's too easy; too hard to resist. Still, it would be nice to get laid a bit more."

John nodded in agreement.

"Oh yeah."

Then, out of the corner of their eyes, they noticed Michael coming through the door at the far end of the hall and spun in their chairs to greet him. A good look at him though - as he slumped into the first chair he came to - revealed that he seemed the worse for wear.

Blood was clear to see around his face and he looked to be in some degree of pain. They both got up and ran across the hall to his aid.

"Are you okay mate? What the fuck happened to you?" asked John.

The concern was obvious in his voice.

"Wrong man in the wrong place at the wrong time," replied Michael.

He was now leaning forward, gripping his left hand with his right.

John was quick to pick up on it.

"What's wrong with your hand?"

"Broken finger."

"Jesus Christ! Who was it Michael? Tell us what fucking happened!"

"Okay, okay."

John and Stuart sat down opposite him to listen.

"I was at the Doom Room on my own, because it's been a bit slow the last few weeks and you wouldn't expect any trouble. There's been nothing since we went down there and saw off those Asian lads.

Anyway, it was all good until I went outside for some air. Actually, I was debating finishing up for the night, even though I hadn't sold out yet. I was just bored of the place, especially on my own.

So I am drinking a bottle of water around the corner, deciding what to do and who comes walking up from a parked car? It's the three Asian guys from before with a couple of mates.

I didn't have time to run or do anything. I managed to connect a couple of decent punches, before I got trailed to the ground and got kicked around by the five of them.

Then, they stopped and I thought it was over. I thought I was okay. But those fuckers twisted my left arm behind my back and snapped one of my fingers. Fucking hell it was sore; I've never felt anything so painful."

"Which finger did they break?" chipped in Stuart.

Almost as soon as the words came out of his mouth, he realised how inappropriate they were and wished he had kept them to himself.

Michael responded accordingly.

"What the fuck does it matter? It was the pinky one! It's one of my fucking fingers fucked for I don't know how long!"

John was absolutely fuming and had heard all he needed to hear. They were all supposed to be brothers and he would have done anything for any of them, but he and Michael had a special bond, after all they'd been through together.

And the guys from before! John couldn't believe it. After what he did to them and the severe physical warning they got the following week, he never thought they'd be back around that club, even just for an innocent night out, let alone to settle a score.

The Brotherhood ruled that club. The tattoo was known and respected. The very audacity of these guys enraged John, almost as much as the nitty-gritty of what they had done to Michael.

He had not been this angry in a long time. In fact, he wasn't sure if he'd ever been this angry. He was ready to kill these guys with his bare hands and wanted to inflict on them one hundred times the pain that they'd inflicted on Michael.

Now he just had to find them.

"Get Michael some ice and painkillers and then wait here with him. I'm going up to tell Doug and get this thing sorted."

Stuart headed towards the kitchen to get ice and strong pain relief tablets, while John charged up to Doug's office, ready to go out and wage war.

NEIL WALKER

Chapter Thirty

Doug was just as incensed as John had been and within five minutes the two of them - as well as Sanjay - were speeding along dark country roads, each of them carrying a loaded handgun. They were all furious and just wanted to get there and get these guys.

They split up as they made their way through the still packed Doom Room. The guy at the door had thought they were insane - paying twelve pounds in for the last ten minutes - but had been sensible enough not to question their seemingly stupid behaviour.

They knew they didn't have long as they marched around the club, shoving people out of the way to speed their search. Three of the guys, all three of them would recognise. The other two, they did not know, but they were hoping and assuming that the five would still be together, working their 'new territory'.

John headed straight for the gents toilets, hoping to find them doing some last minute business. He was in a blind rage as he burst in and quickly looked around the busy toilet area.

There was one Asian guy, stepping away from the urinal, who caught his eye. He was not one of the three that John had dealt with previously, but was he one of the other two? At this point, John was assuming guilt, pending proof of innocence.

He walked straight at the guy, who didn't even notice him coming - as he was still adjusting his belt - and head-butted him squarely on the nose, dropping him down on his knees.

"Are you one of them?" he screamed ferociously, before starting to viciously kick him.

Every time the guy moved his arms to protect himself, John would kick the area left exposed, not stopping for a second. The guy was sliding himself backwards along the ground, in a futile attempt to escape from the constant barrage of blows.

The toilets were mostly cleared of people now, with only a few voyeuristic fight fans hanging around near the door to watch what happened - ready to make a quick escape, if he should turn on them.

Every few seconds, John would keep screaming, "Are you one of them?" while continuing to stomp and kick the guy.

He made it as far as the toilet cubicle, edging backwards across the floor, and tried in vain to get himself in the door and close it on John. He had no such luck and the very idea that the guy was trying to escape him seemed to anger John even more.

After one last stomp on the head - cracking it against the side of the toilet - he bent down, grabbed him by the hair, picked him up on his knees and spun him around, smashing his face against the toilet seat, which had been left up.

He did it three times, before the thick black seat smashed, leaving the guy face down on the cubicle floor, blood all over the toilet and pouring from his face on to the tiles.

Again, John shouted the same thing at him at the top of his voice.

"Are you one of them?"

This time, the guy - still lying face down - reached into one of the pockets of his jeans and pulled out two twenty pound notes. He held them as far into the air as he could, pointing them in John's direction.

He wasn't one of them. It hit John like a wave, as he stepped back, looking at the mess he had made of this random person.

Straight away, Doug - who had just walked in - grabbed him by the shoulder.

"Come on, it's time to go. They're not here and if they were, they've probably seen us before we've seen them and got out. Don't worry John; we'll get them. We will get them."

NEIL WALKER

Chapter Thirty-One

It was Monday evening and John was alone in the gym, working out on the punch bag. He was a sweaty, gasping wreck; leathering punches into it like it had stolen something from him. He had been really pushing himself hard for about half an hour now, with only a couple of short breaks, to prevent him having a heart attack.

Since Saturday night and the incident with Michael, he had been seething and was still full of violent rage. He knew that he would not be content until the people responsible for Michael's injuries were hospitalised or dead.

Doug had been working on tracking them down - he knew that - and Doug had promised him that nothing would be done to the guilty parties without him being present. Despite this knowledge and his belief that Doug was intent on tracking them down, John found it hard to be patient. He wanted the matter resolved immediately - and violently.

It had been quite a motivational force for him in the gym. Sunday and Monday had been possibly the two most intensive days of training he had ever done, in spite of Sunday usually being his day off.

Part of it was just venting his anger and frustration and part of it was wanting to be at his peak for beating the five culprits senseless. He had found it difficult to sleep since the incident, but was running on pure adrenaline, pure desire for revenge.

As he turned away from the punch bag, it seemed the time had come. Sanjay was lingering in the doorway and spoke to him, with no emotion in his voice.

"We've finished looking into the thing with Michael. Come through to the main hall."

John responded immediately, with breathless questions.

"Have you got them? Are they there?"

Sanjay did not respond. He just walked away from the doorway, heading for the main hall.

Without even so much as wiping the sweat from his body, he went straight after Sanjay, pulling his loosely tied gloves off with his teeth and dropping them at his feet as he went. He left his hands wrapped, just in case he needed to protect his knuckles and wrists.

He walked into the hall, just behind Sanjay, to see everyone else standing in a circle in the middle of it. Before he could get to see what was happening in the centre of the circle, he heard an agonised scream coming from it, prompting enthusiastic cheers from those looking on.

John ran up to the circle and pushed past those in his way, eager to get in there. All he could think of was just getting to those guys and letting loose on them. The physical tiredness from his workout was gone and he was glad he'd left his hands strapped up. He was going to make them pay.

As he stepped into the circle, however, he got a major shock. He absolutely couldn't believe it.

The sight before him was that of Michael, taped to a metal chair - face bloodied and filled with anguish and pain - and Doug standing over him, obviously the source of his suffering.

John reacted on an emotional level and before he could attempt to rationalise or even find out what was happening, he lunged at Doug, right fist clenched, ready to halt proceedings.

He didn't quite make it as far as Doug. Sanjay - having followed closely behind him - grabbed him around the throat with his right arm and pulled him back, choking him as he did so.

Doug turned to face him and calmly gave instruction to his lieutenant.

"Not too hard Sanjay, you'll cut off the circulation."

Sanjay loosened his grip slightly and once Doug was content that John wasn't going to be asphyxiated, he began to explain things to him.

"Well John, have I got a story to tell you? I'm sure you're wondering what exactly is going on - why young Michael here is in the process of receiving a very thorough beating and why his family of choice is cheering along.

The answer my friend is simple. We are his brothers and to betray us is to betray himself and put his life in our hands."

Walking up to John, who was still being half strangled by Sanjay, Doug spoke quietly to him.

"That's right Johnny Boy, your friend and mine - a man we'd both trust with our lives - has betrayed us. He has lied to us and stolen from us. But don't take it from me, listen to him."

Doug then turned to Michael and shouted at him, the anger and bitterness evident in his voice.

"Come on Michael, tell him what you told the rest of us!"

Michael looked up and faced John and before he'd said a word, he'd said it all. John could tell by the look in his eyes that it was all true. He knew him too well and his eyes always gave him away.

Despite being in a lot of pain, he managed to speak clearly.

"I'm guilty. Don't feel sorry for me, because I did it. I betrayed you all. I lied. I lied about everything. A few too many sure things that never happened and now look at me. It's my own fault; I was fucking stupid and now I'm fucked."

Doug interrupted Michael at this point, having heard enough from him.

"Yes, he is fucked. You see, we found out exactly who those wannabe gangsters were the last time we dealt with them - names, addresses of relatives, everything. One quick trip to see Ali - the gang leader - at his parents' house, told us all we needed to know. He is in fucking prison and has been for three months.

And we didn't just take their word for it. We tortured them for nearly an hour and still the facts remained.

Ali is banged up and we've been stitched up by this bastard. He barely even denied it either. As soon as we confronted him, he knew he'd been caught.

You see, he had sold out nice and early in The Doom Room and gone back to his flat to relax for a while, before the party. Unfortunately for him, when he got home, some friends of his were waiting for him; the kind of friends who break your finger and take whatever money you've got on you as a down payment. And so began the lies."

John tapped Sanjay's arm, to indicate that he no longer needed to be restrained and - reluctantly - Sanjay let him go.

For John, this was a lot to take on board. He'd spent two days psyched up, ready to kill someone over what happened to Michael. He hadn't been able to sleep.

And now, not only had the whole thing been a tissue of lies, it was clear that Michael had attempted to essentially steal money from the organisation. One of his best friends and his brother by oath had told him barefaced lies. Michael had betrayed him; he had betrayed them all.

He didn't have long to contemplate these revelations, before Doug was back to work. He went around behind Michael and in one hard wrenching motion, pulled back the pinky finger on his right hand - the one that had not previously been broken - snapping it and causing him to let out another scream.

John felt sick. This was hard to watch, nauseating to watch, but what could he do? There was no fighting the inevitable. And by the rules that they all chose to live by, he had brought it on himself.

Never had John really considered one of them doing something like this, let alone Michael; the very person who got him involved in the first place. But by the oath he had taken, his hands were tied. He could do nothing but look on and fight his instinct to intervene, to save his friend, to end this horrendous punishment.

Soon, he had taken a severe beating and had suffered a lot. But had he suffered enough? Was it time to put him out of his misery?

Judging by Doug, ending this was the last thing on his mind. It was obvious he had decided that Michael was to be made an example of. Things were only going to get worse for him.

Speaking loudly, Doug addressed the crowd, who were by now whipped into a perverse frenzy of sadistic pleasure in Michael's painful torment. It seemed no one was considering a merciful end for Michael.

"Okay everyone, believe me when I tell you that you will all see the finale of this show later. For now, I just need everyone to wait here. Sanjay, Simon and John - I'll need your help."

NEIL WALKER

Chapter Thirty-Two

John had hoped he'd get through this without having to get directly involved. It now seemed that was wishful thinking on his part.

Much as he wanted to say 'take someone else', he knew he couldn't. This was to be as much a test of his loyalty as anything else. After all, Michael had brought him to Doug and now was shown up to be a traitor. And so, John did as he was told.

"John, you and Simon usher Michael out the back door and wait with him there. Sanjay, you go with them and keep a gun on the traitor at all times. If he tries to escape, kneecap him. I'll meet you in a couple of minutes."

With that, Doug left the hall and the others dispersed themselves, leaving just John, Simon and Sanjay standing over Michael. As John and Simon began to untie him from the chair, Sanjay took out a .45 automatic and aimed it at his head. There was no way Michael was going to escape. He seemed resigned to his fate though and didn't struggle or try to make a break for it, as they made their way to the back door.

They didn't have to wait long outside, before Doug pulled around in a new looking grey van. John had never seen it before, but Doug always kept the garages locked, so he could have had any number of vehicles in it that he rarely used. Everyone else just parked their cars on the tarmac, at the rear of the house.

Doug stayed seated in the driver's seat of the van, while Sanjay walked over and slid the main door of the rear section open, never taking his eyes - or his gun - off Michael. He then ushered them over and as they approached, it was clear that the van had a lot of hi-tech looking equipment in it.

It reminded John of the vans that undercover cops would use for stakeouts in American movies.

Sanjay stepped in first and stood with his back to all the equipment running along the far side of it. He trained his gun on Michael, as he stepped in, and gave him his instructions.

"Get down on your knees, with your back to the side of the van."

Michael did as he was told, kneeling down with his back to the door side of the van, facing the equipment. John and Simon stepped in and Simon closed the door behind them. They sat on the seats in front of the equipment - which were bolted to the bottom of the van - while Sanjay opted to sit on the floor beside Michael, keeping his gun on him. Doug started driving and so began the journey.

John was filled with a sense of dread at what might be in store for Michael at the end of it. Not knowing was really hard.

He wished he had not been brought along, although given the circumstances there was no way around it. He just decided that all he could do was try his utmost to detach himself from the situation and just deal with it the best he could after the fact.

The only break in the silence during the drive was when Simon decided to switch on one of the TV monitors. On came a snowstorm of noisy static.

The volume had obviously been left up very high and Doug leaned back, like an angry father, shouting at the kids in the back.

"Turn that off and don't touch anything!"

Simon did as he was told.

John knew they must be nearing their destination when Sanjay produced a pair of shiny metal handcuffs from his jacket pocket with his left hand, still keeping the gun on Michael with his right. He threw the cuffs to John, giving him an abrupt order.

"Cuff him to the van."

Under different circumstances, John might have objected to his tone, but that seemed unimportant at this time. He knelt down beside Michael and reached behind him, cuffing his wrists to a fixed metal pole, which ran along the bottom of the door side of the van.

Michael winced slightly, as his hands were obviously very sensitive at this point - each one pained by a broken finger. John didn't apologise, wanting to show no sympathy for his friend at this time. He knew it would do him no favours.

Doug turned around in his seat and with a grin on his face, addressed the Brotherhood members in the back of the van.

"And so it begins."

He really seemed to be relishing his vengeance on Michael.

"Sanjay and Simon, you both know what to do, so let's do it. John, I want you to tape Michael's mouth thoroughly and then watch him. If he runs, you'd better run too, because it's on your head if he's not here when we get back. Apart from guard duty, all you need to do is sit back and watch some reality TV."

Both Sanjay and Simon sniggered at this remark, but John was still very much in the dark. How did Sanjay and Simon know exactly what was going on? And why did he have to be left wondering?

He knew this was not the time for questions, however, and got to work taping Michael's mouth with some elephant tape, handed to him by Sanjay. Meanwhile, Sanjay produced a TV camera from the passenger seat of the van and put it on his right shoulder, switching it on.

John would have been impressed with it - as it was a fully-fledged television camera, not just a camcorder - if he hadn't been so concerned about what was about to happen.

Sanjay was filming Michael cuffed on his knees, bleeding on to the tape that covered his mouth. Simon then got down beside him to get in the shot, producing his Stanley knife, extending the blade and holding it to Michael's throat, while smiling into the camera.

It was hard for John not to just punch him in the face, but to do that would be to cross over, to go from brother to enemy of the family, from friend to foe - basically from alive to dead. So self-control would be the order of the day; he would have to grin and bear it.

The thought of risking everything to save his friend did cross his mind, but what about all his other friends - his brothers by oath? That would mean severing ties with them, leaving his lavish lifestyle, going on the run.

And Michael - Michael had lied to him. He had told him barefaced lies and by his own admission, had betrayed them all. All this was spinning around in his head, while the other three looked all set to get to work.

Sanjay switched on one of the TV monitors and on came Michael's face, the pictures being transmitted from the camera. He then started a tape recording, obviously intending to make a home movie - of sorts.

From the front seat, Doug threw an opened box of women's stockings, having taken one himself already. Simon took one for himself and pulled another one over Sanjay's head, while he continued filming.

Once they all had stockings covering their faces, Sanjay switched on the bright light attached to the front of the TV camera and Simon opened the van door. All three of them stepped out into the dark street, Simon and Doug slamming their respective doors shut behind them.

Now, all both John and Michael could do was look on at the TV screen, dreading what they might be about to see.

Chapter Thirty-Three

It didn't take long for the pictures of Doug and Simon walking along a dimly lit suburban street to ring home with Michael.

He began violently struggling, making heavily muffled screams under the tape and trying to pull himself free. Futile as it was, he was really trying to get loose.

John just continued to watch the TV monitor, not wanting to watch his friend's painful frustration and now even more concerned about what he was going to see. After Michael had seemed so placid and resigned to his fate, he couldn't understand what was making him act like this. Now, John was bracing himself for the absolute worst.

Doug and Simon walked quickly up the driveway of a house, with Sanjay close behind, getting it on camera. Sanjay then stood just filming the front door, while Doug and Simon disappeared around the back.

All that was on the TV screen for almost a full minute was a shot of the varnished door, with the number fifty-seven on it in gold. Then, Simon quickly opened the front door and Sanjay hurried in, closing the door behind him. As Sanjay walked into the living room, capturing the scene before him, John's heart sank. He had been expecting the worst and got it.

Doug was sitting on top of a middle-aged woman, pinning her arms to the ground with his hands. Her mouth had already been taped, but the microphone on the camera could pick up her muted moans.

John knew who she was the second she came into view. He'd seen her picture dozens of times and heard Michael talk about her at length - his mother.

It had been one of their steps along the road of male bonding, discussing their relationships with their mothers, as they had both been part of single-parent families. Michael really did worship his mother and Doug knew him well enough to know this. It seemed he had selected the ultimate punishment for him.

John couldn't look at him now that he knew what was happening and so opted to concentrate on the screen before him, looking on in horror. Simon turned to the camera and waved, before unleashing a violent kick into Moreen's head. John had often, in the past, made fun of Michael's mother's name; claiming it sounded like the name of a 'scrubber', much to his annoyance. Those days were a distant memory now.

Sanjay strategically positioned the camera on the sofa, so that it would capture all the action, but he could get involved. He got down on the floor and helped Simon hold Moreen down, while Doug hoisted up her skirt and viciously tore off her tan tights and her panties.

She was kicking quite a lot at this point, but Doug put an end to that by holding her right leg under his left arm at the knee and pinning her left thigh to the ground with his knee, before delivering a series of powerful punches to her vagina. After this, he let her legs go and there was no more kicking.

He began to unbutton his trousers while Simon - who was holding down her mid-section - ripped open her blouse and pulled up her bra, to reveal her breasts.

His erect penis now exposed, Doug gave Simon a thumbs up before forcing himself inside her. She seemed to have given up struggling now and was just looking blankly up at Sanjay, who was staring directly down at her face, while pinning down her arms.

Michael had far from given up struggling and was still trying for all he was worth to free himself, while moaning through the tape and crying hysterically. John was trying to distance himself as best he could, but considering that he was holding one of his best friends prisoner while they both watched his mother being gang raped it was difficult to do. He kept thinking, what would Michael do? If the roles were reversed, would he give up his whole life - and risk his very existence - to save him?

Sanjay went next, violently thrusting himself inside her again and again. Doug was now pinning down her arms, while Simon continued holding her midsection in place, grabbing at her breasts with one hand.

Letting go of her right arm for a second, Doug slammed a punch into her eye, before pinning down her arm again, as she reached to hold it. It was clear he was out to make it as unpleasant as possible for her.

Michael seemed to have worn himself out, or realised the futility of his struggling. He just lay on his side on the floor of the van sobbing, only occasionally looking up at the screen.

John felt complete revulsion at what he was watching - rape being something he really despised - yet still he watched. Maybe this was because it was too hard to look at or deal with Michael, or maybe he was just watching to see what they were going to do to her next and if they were going to kill her. The fact that they wore stockings over their faces gave John hope that she would live, although they could have just been wearing them to make the ordeal that bit more terrifying for her.

Simon was last to go and got the other two to turn her over, obviously planning to sodomise her. Doug continued holding her arms and Sanjay pressed down on her back, while Simon pulled out his penis and forced it into her. Even with the stocking over his head, John could see he was enjoying it. Simon did relish the more vicious aspects of the job and this was perfect for him.

Continually thrusting in and out, Simon removed his Stanley knife from his jacket pocket and pushed out the blade. Then, just as he was about to climax, he stabbed the sharp blade into her shoulder - narrowly missing Sanjay's hand - and tore it across her back, making a deep and bloody incision, as he ejaculated inside her.

Simon fastened up his trousers and the three of them stood up around her. Doug then kicked her in the ribs and signalled to the other two to start kicking her as well. John continued to watch - while Michael sobbed - wondering when it was going to end.

After the barrage of kicks left her almost unconscious - her broken bleeding body sprawled on the carpet - Doug delivered the final insult. He reached into his still unbuttoned trousers, produced his now limp penis and began urinating on her. It was pouring over her face and on her chest, but she was beyond even holding out her hands to stop it hitting her.

Sanjay picked up the camera - putting it on his shoulder again - and leaned over Moreen, for one final close-up of what they had done. She seemed to be alive - just - and they were finished with her.

They were heading for the front door and removed the stockings from their faces, when the transmission from the camera stopped, it obviously having been switched off.

John just sat there, staring at the static on the screen; not wanting to look away. This had been harrowing, hard to take and totally repulsive, but it wasn't over.

Michael had been given a severe punishment through his mother, but he was still breathing. John knew that would never be the case by the time the night was over.

Chapter Thirty-Four

John did his best to hide his disgust, as the three rapists stepped into the back of the van, but knew it had to be written all over his face. All eyes for now though, were on Michael.

Simon slid the van door closed and Sanjay lifted the camera back on to his shoulder and switched it on. He obviously wanted some reaction footage of Michael, although Michael wasn't exactly giving him a show. He was just lying on his side, staring blankly at the floor.

Doug leaned right down beside him, to say a few choice words.

"Hope you enjoyed that Michael. That my friend is what you get. You fucked with my family, so I fucked with your family - literally.

I must say, your mother wasn't great. I was first in and her cunt was very loose; she must have been a slapper. This is just the start for her now. First the trauma of being gang raped and then the lifetime of stressed out depression that will come from her son disappearing.

She'll spend every day wondering, waiting, getting her hopes up every time the phone rings or there is a knock at the door, hoping it's her son; which of course, it will not be. Tragic really."

Despite this provocation, Michael did not react with anger. He didn't even flinch; far too busy being silently angry with himself to make a pointless struggle against the cuffs to get to Doug.

When a reaction was not forthcoming, Doug went straight out the sliding door - closing it behind him - climbed into the drivers seat and started the van, to get the next leg of the journey under way.

Sanjay switched off the camera, having got the footage he wanted. It seemed obvious to John that the main reason for Doug's little speech to Michael had been to get the point across to the rest of them; don't mess with The Brotherhood or break your oath in any way, or your loved ones are in danger, as are you.

It would work too, although John couldn't think of any of them who would even consider crossing Doug like this. Then again, a few hours previously, he would have said the same of Michael and now he was on his way to be an accomplice to his murder.

This time, Sanjay and Simon sat in the seats and John sat on the floor, near to Michael. He did his best not to look at him, staring at his leg or directly at the floor of the van, trying desperately to detach himself from the reality of what he had done, what he was doing and what he was about to do.

Michael kept the same blank look on his face, not moving or making a sound, as they drove him to his final resting place. Like before, no one was talking, just sitting in silent contemplation.

John looked up at the pair on the seats, to see Sanjay looking very serious, like a machine; doing the job required. Simon, on the other hand, seemed quite smug and almost pleased with himself, fidgeting with his Stanley knife.

He was certainly living up to his reputation. John had felt he was a decent guy to begin with and that perhaps Stuart had exaggerated about his sadistic tendencies, but not any longer.

The van slowed to a halt in a darkened country lane, the same one that they had taken Peter to. Sanjay immediately got back into the role of cameraman, pointing it at Michael, while Simon uncuffed him from the metal pole in the van and cuffed his hands behind his back. The door slid open, to reveal Doug standing looking in, holding a torch in his right hand and a shovel in his left.

"Okay lads, bring him out and let's get this over with."

Simon dragged Michael to his feet and led him out towards Doug, Sanjay close behind, capturing all the emotion of the occasion with the camera.

John was last out of the van and closed the door behind him, stopping for a second - as it slammed in front of him - to wrestle with the situation one more time. This was his last chance to do anything, if that's what he wanted to do. This was his opportunity to save Michael's life.

Although in his gut, he felt like he should, he told himself one last time that Michael had brought this on himself and deserved what he was going to get and that was it. He turned and followed the funeral procession, which was already making its way through the gate, into the dark empty field.

They walked for a good five minutes through the muddy field, with only the light of Doug's torch and the light attached to Sanjay's camera to guide them, before Doug stopped; stabbing the shovel into the ground, leaving the wooden shaft standing straight up in the air, marking the spot.

"Take off his cuffs," was his order to Simon, who swiftly obliged.

As soon as Michael's hands were free, Doug shone the torch on the patch of ground the shovel was stuck in and announced what would happen next.

"Right then Michael, this is the end of the road. It's time to dig. We've got hours of darkness left, so take as long as you like. After all, it's your grave, so make it as deep as you want; you'll be spending a lot of time in it."

Michael stepped forward - his mouth still taped shut - and stood in front of the shovel. He turned to Doug and pointed at the elephant tape preventing any last words, in an attempt to be granted permission to remove it. Doug shook his head, before pointing at the shovel, indicating he should get on with it.

As he began digging, Sanjay moved round in front of him, seemingly wanting to record the look on his face, as he prepared his own grave, on camera.

John wasn't sure what he found more sickening, the things that they were doing to Michael, or the fact that they were capturing them for everyone to enjoy on video. He kept his eyes down and his mouth shut though, giving nothing away.

Simon took off his jacket, laying it down on the ground and sitting on it, making himself comfortable. He then offered some sarcastic encouragement.

"Come on mate, put your back into it! It's not gonna dig itself!"

Michael seemed to be digging forever, as the grave grew gradually deeper, while they all looked on, patiently waiting. His pace had not been helped by the fact that he had a broken finger on each hand.

It was at least three or four feet deep by now though - definitely deep enough - and John couldn't help but wonder if Michael was prolonging these last minutes of his life, not wanting to turn, drop the shovel and indicate that it was time.

Was he playing back the highlights of his life in his head, or merely re-living the horror of the previous couple of hours? John would have the rest of his life to wonder, as Michael would be given no last words.

Although he took his time over the task, it still came as a shock when he eventually stopped digging and dropped the shovel, looking up to signal his demise.

"Throw up the shovel," was all Doug had to say, as he moved into position, facing down on Michael.

Michael obliged, seeming to have no heart left for any confrontation. He was ready for the end.

Doug produced a .22 with a silencer on it and, aiming it with his right hand - still holding the torch in his left - he fired ten shots in quick succession, into Michael's legs. He dropped on his back, writhing in pain, as Doug paused to reload.

Sanjay was leaning over him with the camera, making sure he got the ending of his homemade snuff movie. John and Simon were also stood over the grave, watching their friend as he wriggled in the mud, his dignity and will to live having deserted him.

After reloading, Doug opened fire again, firing five shots into his right arm and shoulder and five into his left. He then placed the weapon in his pocket, giving instructions to John and Simon.

"You two, fill him in."

He was still alive. He was blatantly in a huge amount of pain and not far away from death, but he was still alive. John wanted to scream for reason, for mercy, or for something. How horrific did this have to be?

Simon, on the other hand, had no problems with the order and immediately picked up the shovel and got to work, slapping the mud down on their bloodied friend - their brother.

If he'd wanted to stop this, his chance had come and gone a long time ago. Aware that the camera was on him and that Michael would die more quickly if they filled him in as swiftly as possible, John began kicking over the mounds of mud that surrounded the hole in the ground, speeding up the burial.

It took only a few minutes, despite the depth of the grave, and they were soon making their way back to the van, each engrossed in their own thoughts, John trying not to think at all.

NEIL WALKER

Chapter Thirty-Five

It had only been eight months, though it seemed so much longer, only eight months since he returned from Australia, only eight months since it all began, but now it had to end and John knew it.

The prospect of existing outside the bubble of The Brotherhood was a daunting one. This violent drug gang had come to include his friends, his home, his whole support system, his money, his gym - everything.

He had placed all his eggs in one basket and now the rot had set in and he would have to deal with it.

But if starting again was daunting - beginning a new chapter in his life - then bringing this one to a close was even more so.

The video had been very popular viewing, from that night when they got back, right through the week. He had seen it maybe ten times and he'd been trying to avoid it.

And the viewings were not sombre ones, with everyone regretful of what 'had to happen', no. There had been laughter, vulgar attempts at humour being shouted at the screen - a good excuse for drinking and fast food.

He had played the role, giving nothing away, mirroring the behaviour of those around him; so as not to arouse suspicion for what was to come.

He'd worked and partied both Friday and Saturday nights and not even Stuart could have spotted anything amiss, although he had been very evasive with Stuart, when he would try to instigate conversation about Michael. There was only so much he could pretend.

Still, none of them knew how he felt and none of them suspected a thing. But they would know, they would all soon know the extent of his anger.

Doug, Sanjay and Simon had gone way too far. The Brotherhood had gone way too far. What they had done that night, to Michael and to his mother, was over the top beyond all measure in John's eyes. And the fact that they had videoed it and were all still watching it for recreation he found totally sickening and infuriating.

Of course, a lot of his anger had been directed at himself and that would be something he would be dealing with long after The Brotherhood was a distant memory.

The guilt plagued him day and night; guilt he hoped might be eased slightly by vengeance - Michael's vengeance, delivered by him.

After a couple of days, it had come to him; a simple plan, which would avenge Michael and give him a way out, and now it had to be done.

It had to be now, as he could pretend no longer, look these people in the eye and smile no longer, watch Michael's video and smirk no longer.

Now was the time.

Very rarely did anyone make use of the magnificent grounds surrounding the house, apart from the occasional game of football, on the patch of grass nearest the building.

Having spent the afternoon walking around them, John regretted not having done it more often, for this would surely be his last opportunity. However, he had more pressing regrets on his mind.

As he stepped into the house, the reality of what he was about to do was still sinking in, but he knew he had to follow through his plan; he knew it was the only way now.

Whether or not he'd feel any better about himself after he'd done it, he didn't know, but he had to see it through.

NEIL WALKER

Chapter Thirty-Six

He had been waiting for almost half an hour, the safe having only taken him a couple of minutes to locate. Doug hadn't been too creative in selecting its location; obviously never expecting this day would come. Picking the lock of the office had been easy; a skill John had learned as a teenager in Belfast, which he had not forgotten. He had locked the door behind him, so as not to arouse suspicion and when he heard Doug's key rattle into the lock, he stood back against the wall, behind the door, realising that the time was at hand.

Both Doug and Sanjay entered through the door - Sanjay closing it behind them - and made their way to the desk, without having noticed the intruder. John cleared his throat to announce his presence and they both spun around to see him standing, aiming two .45s at them; one in each hand.

Sanjay - who was of no particular use to John at this point - reached into his inside pocket for the gun he happened to be carrying and was shot in the head; a perfect shot between the eyes, with the .45 in John's right hand. He felt no remorse whatsoever, as this huge violent man dropped to the ground before him, his own .45 in his hand, just too slow to make a difference.

Doug made no such mistake, holding out his hands, indicating that he was not armed and would be making no attempt to fight back.

"Do you know Doug, there's something I've been meaning to talk to you about and haven't really got around to it, till today."

"What's that?" replied Doug, trying to seem calm, but not doing an incredibly convincing job. He was more than a little bit nervous, having seen Sanjay die in front of him, and John knew it.

"It's your film collection Doug. I mean kudos on having your own cinema, and you do have quite a large collection of celluloid, but Doug, where's the John Woo? In my opinion, the greatest director of all time - certainly the best action director. You've got Sergio Leone, Sam Peckinpah, Martin Scorsese, Don Siegel, but no fucking John Woo. Where's you taste man?

Most people like The Killer or A Better Tomorrow II the best - The Killer is certainly the critics' choice - but my favourite is Hard Boiled."

John fired two shots from each pistol into Doug's kneecaps, dropping him screaming to the ground. Ignoring the cries of pain, John continued talking, as if nothing had happened, slowly stepping towards Doug.

"Hard Boiled was his last Hong Kong movie and I think he wanted to push things as far as they could go. That for me is the best action movie of all time, bar none. Forget The Wild Bunch, forget Dirty Harry, forget fucking Die Hard, this is the one."

John was now standing over Doug and looking down as he spoke.

"He invented the whole thing of shooting two .45s at once you know. It's commonplace in loads of action movies now, but he was the first to do it. It's simple, but very effective.

So Doug, here I am with my two .45s. I'm Chow Yun Fat and you're the bad guy; you're a very fucking bad guy. Not that I'm claiming to be a good guy, far from it. I'm just another bad guy, with a little bit more morality than you. Now is the time to pay for your sins, so I just need you to tell me one thing - "

John walked around behind Doug's desk and swung the wooden door on the right hand side of it open, to reveal a poorly concealed, in-built safe.

"What's the combination?"

Doug did not answer - continuing to yell with pain - and John marched back over to him, delivering a ferocious stomp to his wounded right kneecap. This produced a louder, more agonised yell and John angrily screamed his question at him.

"What's the fuckin' combination you cunt?"

Through the pain, Doug replied with a question of his own.

"Is this about Michael?"

John stepped back and laughed for a second, before reverting to his furious expression and shouting his response.

"Yes it's about Michael, you sick fucking bastard!"

He then stood on his right kneecap again, this time forcing all his weight down on it and holding it; sustaining the pressure.

Again, this brought another agonised scream, but instead of releasing the pressure, John held his foot in place and added to Doug's torment by firing a .45 shot into his left foot, before repeating his question.

"What's the combination?"

Doug stood up to being tortured particularly badly in John's view, considering the tough mindset he preached and the dismissive way he would talk about people who would give up information under duress.

Within fifteen minutes, John had the combination and opened the safe to reveal a lot of cash - obviously at least a couple of week's takings - as well as bags of ecstasy pills, speed and coke. A lot of money and a pile of drugs, as John had hoped.

He had brought two empty sports bags with him, one of which he had already filled with Doug's precious log books and any other paper work he could find in the office. He now began hastily filling the other with the contents of the safe, aware that he was running low on time.

Everyone else had gone to the England game, but would be back soon, as it was after six o'clock. He'd had the perfect excuse not to go - being the only non-English person among them - and had taken full advantage of his opportunity. Having now done what he had to do, he certainly did not want to be there when they all got back.

The money and drugs filled the second sports bag to capacity, except for one bundle of cash, which he shoved into his jacket pocket. Throwing the bags over his shoulder, he then stepped around for his final confrontation with Doug. He was still moaning with pain, but had not lost consciousness and looked straight up at John as he stood over him, taking aim with a .45.

"Are you gonna kill me John, after all I've done for you? How can you kill me? You're just like me."

"At least I'm not making you dig your own grave," were his parting words, before he fired two shots into Doug's head.

Effectively, bringing the leader and his lieutenant to an end meant bringing The Brotherhood to an end. Everything was organised by and channelled through them, so no Doug and Sanjay, no Brotherhood. This was John's reasoning anyway.

John felt that taking the logbooks and paperwork, as well as all the money and drugs, made it virtually impossible for the remaining members of The Brotherhood to continue to operate without Doug and Sanjay, if they would even consider trying.

John had never really warmed to Sanjay, but he had definitely bonded with Doug. It felt weird for him to kill someone he had in some ways been quite close to, or as close as he had been allowed to get.

Indeed, right up until the incident with Michael, John had been fully subscribing to the idea that they were all brothers, all a family, so even though he had come to be disgusted with Doug and Sanjay, he took no pleasure in killing them.

He smiled to himself as he left the office for the last time though, thinking of how Michael would have enjoyed his final revenge.

John was not a religious man - he never had been. As soon as he'd reached the point in his life where he was old enough to think for himself, he had become an atheist. All religion seemed absurd to him and he subscribed very strongly to German philosopher Friedrich Nietzsche's assertion that 'God is dead'.

Despite his lack of religious belief, picturing the image of Michael looking down on him and nodding his approval was comforting to him. It was nice to imagine that Michael got the last laugh, even though The Brotherhood had taken his life.

NEIL WALKER

Chapter Thirty-Seven

John filled the tall glass right to the top, with the iced coffee flavoured milkshake he had become infatuated with, during his first visit to Australia.

After three months back in the country, his taste for it showed no sign of waning - two litres a day being his usual level of consumption. It amused him that this was now his only addiction, his only regular habit.

He had cut his drinking way down and hadn't touched drugs since leaving the UK, opting instead to get his head together, to plan for the future.

He took his drink out on to the balcony, leaving the sliding door open, so he could hear the intercom.

After months of seeing it every day, the view he had still dazzled him, as he looked out across Circular Quay. As far as he was concerned, the Opera House and the Harbour Bridge would never become boring.

He sat down on one of the two metal chairs, which were positioned at either side of the small metal table that graced his balcony, and sipped on his iced coffee, savouring the flavour of his first drink of the day.

He looked at his watch and it was just coming up to twelve noon. Only five hours until he could phone his mother, before she went to work.

He called her religiously every day and had done since the day he arrived back in Australia. He actually spoke to her a lot more at this point, than he ever had when he lived in the UK.

The regular telephone calls were more out of concern for her safety, than a sense of duty, or a real need to talk to her, but she seemed to like it.

The idea of having relatives who were vulnerable back at home pained him, but now he felt like if something were going to happen to them, it would have happened already.

Besides, he very seriously doubted that The Brotherhood would have the means to track them down without Doug and Sanjay, if it was even still in existence.

None of them knew anything about John's life in Belfast and he thought it very unlikely that they would be brave enough to go into a Northern Ireland housing estate to try to do something, even if they did find the house.

Despite this, it did still prey on his mind from time to time.

The buzz of the intercom brought John to his feet, the person he was expecting seeming to have arrived.

He pressed the button to answer.

"Yeah?"

"It's Blair," was the reply.

John pressed the button marked with a key, to let him into the building. He then opened up the apartment door and took a seat at the breakfast bar, setting his iced coffee in front of him.

Blair entered, wearing a tight military green vest top and a pair of tan combat shorts, looking impressively muscular for a nineteen year old and with a tan that looked like he'd been sunbathing - without sunscreen - every day of his life.

"Come in Blair and take a seat," said John.

He then pulled out the seat beside him, for Blair to sit on.

Blair shook his hand as he sat down.

"Good to meet you. Peter talks about you a lot."

"Well, I won't ask what he's been saying."

Blair laughed.

"It's all good, don't worry."

"Okay, so Peter tells me you're well into the club scene in Sydney, is that right?"

"Oh yeah. Every Friday and Saturday night I'm out, without fail. I love my techno."

"Don't we all Blair, don't we all. Peter has also been telling me you're a bit of a tough guy. Is that also true?"

"I can handle myself," Blair replied.

The way he carried himself coupled with the confidence of his answer gave John the impression that he probably could.

"That's what I like to hear. Do you want a drink, by the way; iced coffee, juice, light beer?"

"What beer have you got?"

"Hahn Light."

"Yeah, that's great."

John made his way to the fridge and produced a bottle of Hahn Light, opening it with the bottle opener on the counter. As he set it in front of Blair on the breakfast bar, Blair came to the point - as John might have in a similar situation.

"So, what do you want me to do? Peter said I should see you if I want to get work, but he didn't say what I'd have to do."

"And yet you're here."

"Peter tells me the money is good."

John smiled, already feeling like Blair was the man for the job and opened up one of the kitchen drawers, producing a plastic bag filled with two hundred white pills, which he placed on the breakfast bar beside the beer.

Chapter Thirty-Eight

Gloria was thirty-two and coming mercifully close to the end of her current career. Her husband had just been promoted at work and was now on a fairly impressive salary, so she hoped that when she finished up her career as an air hostess, he would be making enough money to support them both financially.

She had always prided herself on being a strong, confident, independent woman and had made a point of maintaining her career and her independence after she got married. Now she had reached a stage in her life where being a strong, independent, career-minded woman didn't seem quite so important anymore.

Coffee mornings and daytime TV would seem like paradise - as far as she was concerned - compared to the monotony of life as a glorified waitress.

She had reached the point where it was a struggle to put on that 'have a nice day' fake smile, or stand at the front of the plane pointing out the exits and pretending to inflate a life jacket, while everybody giggled or tried not to. Every rude or difficult passenger could be the one to send her over the edge and get a tray of hot airplane food in the face.

This is why she enjoyed working in first class, as usually people would be so comfortable and happy at being pampered, that they would be on their best behaviour, in contrast to the disgruntled economy class passengers; squashed in and irritable.

Today, however, one guy was really getting on her nerves - arrogant and cocky, possessing no manners.

She had her suspicions that he'd been upgraded from economy class, as he wasn't dressed like the average first class passenger and was only maybe twenty-two or twenty-three years old at most, but this didn't matter.

If someone was in the first class section, with a first class ticket, it made no difference if they had paid the full first class fair, or been upgraded from economy. Her job was to treat them all the same and make them feel first class.

She had no way to know for sure anyway, as once they were on the plane, there was no way to tell what their original booking details had been.

On the flight from London to Sydney, there was an extended opportunity for annoyance and there were still eleven hours of flying to go, as the young man beckoned her again by clicking his fingers and looking directly at her.

She couldn't even force the traditional smile, as she walked over.

"Can I help you?" she asked, in as pleasant a tone as she could manage.

"Are these all the films you have on?" he replied.

He held up the in-flight listings magazine, open at the appropriate page.

"Yes, I'm afraid it is," she said.

She turned to walk away, so as to avoid listening to any complaints about the films available.

He called her back though, before she had a chance to get away.

"While you're here, you might as well get me another beer."

She turned back to him and despite wanting to throw him out the door of the plane, maintained a veneer of calm and gave a polite reply.

"Of course Mr. Pollack, which beer would you like?"

"My father's Mr. Pollack. You my love can call me Simon."

THE END

NEIL WALKER

I hope you have enjoyed this novel. Please take a moment to leave a review on Amazon.

Reviews are a critical factor in the success of any novel and are a powerful buying tool to help readers find the right book. As an author, I really appreciate it when readers review my work and I very much enjoy reading their thoughts.

To leave a review, just go to the Amazon page for Drug Gang and then click on 'write a customer review'.

And if you want to see how the Drug Gang story continues, the details of the second and third books in the series are on the following pages.

Many thanks,

Neil Walker

PART TWO OF THE DRUG GANG TRILOGY AVAILABLE NOW!

Drug Gang Vengeance: Drug Gang Part II
by Neil Walker

THE DRUG GANG IS BACK!

IT'S TIME TO PAY FOR YOUR SINS…

Drug Gang Vengeance is the bestselling crime thriller sequel to Drug Gang.

John Kennedy is on his way out of a life of crime in Sydney, when he is hunted down by drug gang The Brotherhood. This leads to a spiral of vengeance and violence that stretches right around the globe…

SECOND PART OF THE DRUG GANG TRILOGY.

NEIL WALKER

PART THREE OF THE DRUG GANG TRILOGY AVAILABLE NOW!

Drug Gang Takedown: Drug Gang Part III
by Neil Walker

ALL BAD THINGS MUST COME TO AN END…

THIS TIME IT'S WAR!

Drug Gang Takedown is the third crime thriller in the bestselling Drug Gang series.

Former drug dealer John Kennedy returns to Sydney to collect the money he is owed, to start a new life. Despite his best efforts to leave the drug world in the past, he quickly finds himself caught in the middle of the biggest drug war in Australian history…

FINAL PART OF THE DRUG GANG TRILOGY.

NEIL WALKER

ABOUT THE AUTHOR

Neil Walker is the bestselling Belfast author of hard-hitting crime fiction. His works include the acclaimed crime thriller Drug Gang and its sequel Drug Gang Vengeance.

Both of these controversial bestsellers are part of the Drug Gang Trilogy and are set in the drug dealing underworld of Manchester, Sydney and Belfast in the early 2000s.

Neil is currently working on the third and final Drug Gang novel. Drug Gang Takedown will be published on 31 January 2019.

To learn more, visit the author's social media pages:

twitter.com/neilwalkerwrote

facebook.com/neilwalkerauthor

instagram.com/neilwalkerauthor

#DrugGang
#DrugGangVengeance
#DrugGangTakedown
#DrugGangTrilogy

Lightning Source UK Ltd.
Milton Keynes UK
UKHW011824290722
406581UK00001B/317

9 781720 207283